Lopez, Barry
Holstun.

Resistance.

$18.00

DATE			

ALSO BY BARRY LOPEZ

Nonfiction

Arctic Dreams

Of Wolves and Men

Fiction

Light Action in the Caribbean

Lessons from the Wolverine

Field Notes

Crow and Weasel

Winter Count

River Notes

Giving Birth to Thunder

Desert Notes

Essays

About This Life

Apologia

The Rediscovery of North America

Crossing Open Ground

Anthology

Vintage Lopez

RESISTANCE

with monotypes by Alan Magee

RESISTANCE

BARRY LOPEZ

Alfred A. Knopf NEW YORK 2004

THIS IS A BORZOI BOOK
PUBLISHED BY ALFRED A. KNOPF

Copyright © 2004 by Barry Holstun Lopez

All rights reserved under International and Pan-American
Copyright Conventions. Published in the United States
by Alfred A. Knopf, a division of Random House, Inc.,
New York, and simultaneously in Canada by Random
House of Canada Limited, Toronto. Distributed by
Random House, Inc., New York.

www.aaknopf.com

Knopf, Borzoi Books, and the colophon are registered
trademarks of Random House, Inc.

Book design by Virginia Tan

Library of Congress Cataloging-in-Publication Data
Lopez, Barry Holstun, [date]
    Resistance / Barry Lopez—1st ed.
      p. cm.
    ISBN 1-4000-4220-8 (alk. paper)
    1. Psychological fiction, American.   2. Government,
resistance to—Fiction.   3. Life change events—Fiction.
4. Political fiction, American.   5. Counterculture—
Fiction.   I. Title.
PS3562.O67R47 2004
813'.54—dc22   2003065986

Manufactured in the United States of America
First Edition

The titles of the monotypes in this work are:

Writer's Mask, page 2; *Silence,* page 20; *Wound,* page 38;
Dulce et Decorum Est, page 54; *The Animals,* page 70;
Spirit, page 90; *The Lamb,* page 112; *Wind,* page 126;
Dialogue of Comfort, page 142. They have been previously
published in *Archive: Alan Magee Monotypes* (Darkwood
Press & Spectrum Concerts, Berlin, 2000) Copyright
© 2000 by Alan Magee; and *Alan Magee: Paintings,
Sculpture, Graphics* (Forum Gallery, New York, 2003)
Copyright © 2003 by Alan Magee.

For Amanda, Stephanie, Mary, and Mollie

CONTENTS

Author's Note   ix

Apocalypse   3

Río de la Plata   21

Mortise and Tenon   39

Traveling with Bo Ling   55

The Bear in the Road   71

The Walls at Yogpar   91

Laguna de Bay in A-Sharp   113

Niłch'i   127

Flight from Berlin   143

AUTHOR'S NOTE

The monotypes in *Resistance* are from a larger body of work created by Alan Magee between 1990 and 2000. A few of the earliest images were included in a show of the artist's work at the Staempfli Gallery in New York in the fall of 1990. The full collection was presented for the first time at the Berliner Philharmonic in Berlin in November 2000.

I would like to thank Alan and Monika Magee for their conversation and hospitality while I was at work on *Resistance,* and also Marion Gilliam for his gracious support. Luis Verano, Isabel Sterling, Skip Cosper, and T. R. Hummer helped me clarify several fine points in the stories, and I'm most grateful.

RESISTANCE

Apocalypse

I remember the morning the letter came. I left the apartment Mary and I were renting on rue Lepic and strolled in the sunshine up to rue des Abbesses. The old sidewalks were freshly washed, the air was still cool. My regular way was to get a morning paper, a brioche, and black coffee and then sit in the little park by the Métro station and read. Sometimes I would walk up Yvonne-le-Tac to the terraced park below Sacré-Coeur instead, but that morning I had that fistful of mail.

We took the apartment partly because it was right around the corner from the cemetery in Montmartre. Mary was writing an essay about the cemeteries of France for *Harper's,* a history of how they had been disrupted and desecrated by revolution, by the expansion of cities, and of course by the Church. The Cimetière de Montmartre was palpable, a reassurance to her. Many of its graves had been destroyed in 1789, the bodies treated like so

much trash by those who hated royalty and aristoc-
racy, and by the hoodlums who always attach themselves to social change. But Degas is buried there,
the composer Berlioz, Nijinsky, and her favorite,
Adolphe Sax, the inventor of the saxophone.

It was not these ghosts, though, nor the untrou-
bled *allées* colonnaded by plane trees, that calmed
her. It was that the stillness sheltered an aggrega-
tion of mute evidence, apparent throughout the
city in its small-scale neighborhoods, that our history is finally human. Regimes and ideologies—
Tamerlane's Mongol empire, Caligula's Rome,
Stalin's Soviet Union—whatever their horrors,
whatever afflictions they deliver, pass away. What
endures is simple devotion to the question of
having been alive. The cemetery comforted her
because it was not about death but about transcendent joie de vivre.

One day she returned to the apartment and read
me an inscription she'd copied from a gravestone.
Ma gracieuse épouse . . . A husband had expressed
his love and regard for his wife of fifty-one years in
a few bare, unselfconscious sentences. Mary sat
with the piece of paper in her hand by the open
window, watching patrons in the bistro across the
street talking and hailing friends passing on the
sidewalk, and turned a shoulder so I could not see
her crying.

Her tears, I thought, were over a kind of loss we

had talked about in recent weeks, the way the fabric of love scorches, no matter how vigilant we are. The intricate nature of the emotions men and women exchange made the two of us sense our own endangerment when we disagreed; but we had also been speaking of the ephemeral love one can feel toward a complete stranger, for the way they step off a sidewalk or a father hands his daughter her gloves at the door. Bound together in these many ways we are still swept suddenly out of each other's lives, by tides we don't recognize and tides we do. The sensation of loss, the weight of grief, the feeling of being naked to a menace are hard to separate. The fear of an outside force at work makes us reticent in love, and suspicious. We identify enemies.

The instruments of discord show up daily in our lives, of course, demanding our attention. The unscrupulous peer, the woman on the make, the purblind enforcer, the self-anointed official and his cronies, people with a craving for confrontation. We are foolish to give any of them what they ask for, and we betray ourselves and anyone toward whom we have ever felt tender by not sending such people immediately on their way.

The first two pieces of mail I opened that morning were letters from museums, one in Rouen, the other in Orléans. At the time, I was trying to assemble work by European artists which had been shaped by their experience with *le Maquis,* the French underground, for a show to open at the Walker Art Center in Minneapolis and then to travel around the United States. The communications were about insuring the works the museums were lending. I read each one with relief as, sentence by sentence, they eliminated the risks on my part. I should have known—the consideration.

The rest of the mail was personal—friends and family, some items of business for Mary. The one letter I put off reading sat all the while on the green slats of the bench while I finished perusing the paper. The envelope had the look of something you might be sent by the Internal Revenue Service, carrying news of an irregularity in your filings, a notice of additional tax due, perhaps a penalty. But the letter was from another federal authority, a branch of our government but a few years old though already monolithic. Its special charge was to make the nation safe from attack by a great array of vaguely defined "terrorists," domestic and foreign. This work it pursued with religious fervor and special exemptions from the Department of Justice.

I read the letter twice, concealed it in the half fold of *Le Monde,* and walked back to the apartment. Mary was in her robe, making breakfast. I handed her the letter and took her place at the stove.

She read it in the chair by the window.

"I will never get used to this hyperbolic crap," she said, folding the letter back up. "Every fascist step they take, you expect people to laugh in their faces, just take their toys away, you know—the guns and the new laws. Do they just not register the suspicion, the resentment in half the streets in the world?"

She turned abruptly to look out the window, as if responding to someone down there on the sidewalk. Incomprehension, exhaustion, fear passed behind her eyes. She let the letter drop to the floor as if it were an advertising circular.

"I can't believe we have to take people like this seriously, Owen."

I put breakfast on the table, refreshed her coffee, and came back with my laptop. I began e-mailing a loose network of people I'd been in regular touch with since the change of administration took place in our country. We communicated through a series of codes and used electronic back doors which delayed exchanges, but by mid-morning I'd confirmed what I had suspected. The letter had gone to everyone.

It came from Inland Security, the group of people we had come to call the Idiots of Light, for the way they are dazzled by their god. Their ranks include people who celebrate the insults of advertising and the deceptions of public relations cam-

paigns as paths to redemption. The letter also orig-
inated with the Division of Economic Equality,
those in the Department of Commerce we call the
Lottery Enforcers, who argue for the calming and
salutary effect of regular habits of purchase. And it
bore the gold, eagle-talon insignia of the Delta
Confederacy, the contingent of citizen groups that
reports to the education staff of the Office of
Inland Security.

The letter's authors informed us of the nation's
persisting need for democratic reform. Each of us
was told of widespread irritation with our work,
and the government's desire to speak with us.

The authority behind the letter—two crisply
printed cream-colored sheets of laid paper with sig-
natures in red ballpoint—made my breath shud-
der. I sat watching for incoming e-mail. We hadn't
anticipated this, not exactly this frontal an
approach.

After university I and my friends had scattered
abroad—to Brussels, Caracas, Sapporo, Mel-
bourne, Jakarta, any promising corner. Two or three
went deep upriver on the Orinoco or out onto the
plateaus of Tibet and Ethiopia. We had come to
regard the work of writers and artists in our country
as too compliant, as failing to expose or indict the
escalating nerve of corporate institutions, the

increasing connivance of government with business, or the cowardice of those reporting the news.
In the 1970s and '80s, we thought of our artists and
writers as people gardening their reputations, while
the families of our neighborhoods disintegrated
into depression and anger, the schools flew apart,
and species winked out. It was the triumph of adolescence, in a nation that wanted no part of its
elders' remonstrance or any conversion to their
doubt.

The years passed. We had no plan. We had no
hope. We had no religion. We had faith. It was our
belief that within the histories of other, older cultures we would find cause not to be incapacitated
by the ludicracy of our own. It was our intuition
that even in those cultures into which our own had
injected its peculiar folklore—that success is financial achievement, that the future is better, that life
is an entertainment—we would encounter enduring stories to trade in. We thought we might be
able to discern a path in stories and performances
rooted in disparaged pasts that would spring our
culture out of its adolescence.

This remains to be seen. We stay in close touch
(a modern convenience), scattered though we are.
And now others, of course, keep close watch on us,
on what we write and say, on whom we see. We are
routinely denounced by various puppet guards at
home, working diligently for a prison system we

don't believe in. As the days have mounted, though, we've tasted more of the metal in that system's bars.

We feel cold.

Our goal is simple: we want our country to flourish. Our dilemma is simple: we cannot tell our people a story that sticks. It is not that no one believes what we say, that no one knows, that none of our countrymen cares. It is not that their outspoken objections have been silenced by the rise at home of local cadres of enforcement and shadow operatives. It is not that they do not understand. It is that they cannot act. And the response to tyranny of every sort, if it is to work, must always be this: dismantle it. Take it apart. Scatter its defenders and its proponents, like a flock of starlings fed to a hurricane.

Our strategy is this: we believe if we can say what many already know in such a way as to incite courage, if the image or the word or the act breaches the indifference by which people survive, day to day, enough will protest that by their physical voices alone they will stir the hurricane.

We're not optimistic. We chip away like coolies at the omnipotent and righteous façade, but appear to ourselves as well as others to be ineffective dissenters. We've found nothing to use against tyranny that has not been written down or danced out or sung up ten thousand times. It is the somnolence, the great deafness, that reveals our problems. It is illiteracy. It is an appetite for distraction, which has become a cornerstone of life in our nation. In distraction one encounters the deaf. In utter distraction one discovers the refuge of illiteracy.

And here is nearly the bitterest of blunt issues for us: What can love offer that cannot be rejected? What gesture cannot be maligned as witless by those who strive for every form of isolation? When we were young, each of us believed that to love was to die. Then we believed that to love was essential. Now we believe that without love our homeland— perhaps all countries—will perish. Over the years, as we have learned what it might mean to love, we have generally agreed that we've better understood the risks. In our nation, it is acceptable to resent love as an interference with personal liberty, as a ruse the emotions employ before the battlements of reason. It is the abused in our country who now most weirdly profess love. For the ordinary person, love is increasingly elusive, imagined as a strategy.

We reject the assertion, promoted today by success-mongering bull terriers in business, in government, in religion, that humans are goal-seeking animals. We believe they are creatures in search of proportion in life, a pattern of grace. It is balance and beauty we believe people want, not triumph. The stories the earth's peoples adhere to with greatest faith—the dances that topple fearful walls; the ethereal performances of light, color, and music; the enduring musics themselves—are all well patterned. And these templates for the maintenance of vision, repeated continuously in wildly different idioms, from the eras of Lascaux and Shanidar to the days of the Prado and Butoh, these patterns from the artesian wells of artistic impulse, do not require updating. They require only repetition. Repetition, because just as murder and infidelity are within us, so, too, is forgetfulness. We forget what we want to mean. To achieve progress, we've all but cut our heads off.

We found the Inland Security letter ridiculous, but also alarming. It declared that, as none of us had renounced his or her citizenship, we would be interrogated as nationals "with the full cooperation of the stewards of democracy in your host countries." We might then be indicted; or dismissed and ignored; or possibly turned over to local authorities, "some of whom," we were advised, "might have no regard for due process, the writ of habeas corpus, or other advancements in law which are found in civilized countries." The disposition of our cases, it was made clear, would not be at our discretion.

Our stratagems, the letter continued, were those typical of "terrorist cells." They called for scrutiny; and we had to desist. We were reminded, then, not any longer to circulate those texts, images, music, and films already listed as anti-democratic in monthly bulletins from the Select Committee on the Arts, an innovation of the Offices of the President. Or any artistic or literary works created by cultures "inimical to our nation's policies." To achieve wealth, the letter informed us, is the desire of all peoples everywhere; and while our nation was working to establish wealth for all peoples everywhere, resistance like ours, a quibbling over methods, actually created poverty.

The letter explained, in phrases that bore the brushstrokes of zealots and lawyers, that we were to be sought out, quizzed, and possibly punished or isolated from society, because we "were terrorizing the imaginations of our fellow citizens" with our books, paintings, and performances. Sojourning, some of us, with "unadvanced" cultures, attending to their myths and stories, along with making inquiries into primitive or revolutionary art, had poisoned our capacity to understand civilization's triumphs. We were attempting to resurrect the past and have it stand equal with the present. We profoundly misunderstood, our accusers argued, the promise of the future. We were offering only darkness where for some centuries the fires of freedom had been blazing, the beacons of prosperity increasing in their intensity.

The letter implied that there was still hope for us, however. The interrogations, the extraditions, trials, and incarcerations—these need not follow a predictable course. Apology, if of the most profound sort, was a possibility. Reeducation was an option. Missionary work, yet another possibility. In a democracy, the acknowledgment of one's errors, coupled with a suitable penance, could leave an individual with a very bright future. Some, inevitably, would have to face harsh punishment for fooling with the country's destiny.

The human imagination, the letter speculated, was a problematic force, its use best left to experts. An imagination in the wrong hands, missing the guidance of democratic reasoning and fed the wrong ideas, an imagination with no measure of economic awareness, was a loose cannon.

The combustible nature of the communiqué, its rhetorical gibberish, its Draconian suspicions, its headlong theorizing, its fear of contradiction were all of a piece—fundamentalism's rave and cant. That our government had succeeded in reaching each of us with such a letter, considering the deluge of volunteers among domestic antiterrorist groups who had responded to its call for administrative help, was no surprise. What surprised us was that we mattered to this degree, that we represented a serious threat.

The dispatch, then, made us think. It made us wonder if that leap of faith by which we had lived each day, and according to which every citizenry would outlive its tyrants, was not a more valid belief than we had supposed.

The contents of the letter galvanized each of us. In that small apartment on rue Lepic that morning, Mary and I made a decision, which we then communicated to our friends in Alice Springs and elsewhere. When we had read their responses, we packed.

We are not to be found now. We have unraveled ourselves from our residences, our situations. But like a bulb in a basement, suddenly somewhere we will turn on again in darkness. We will carry what we know—what it can mean to have your country under you like a hammock, what it is to take part in the world instead of using your people as fodder in a war to control the world's meaning and expression—we'll carry all of this into other countries. It will be hidden in our individual skills, in our dress, our speech and manner, in the memory of each one of us. The memory of one will kindle the memory of another, a burst of electricity across a chasm. We will disrupt through witness, remembrance, and the courtship of the imagination. We will escort children past the darkest warrens of the forest. We will construct kites that stay aloft in the rain. We will champion what is beautiful, and so finally make our opponents irrelevant.

For all we know our interrogators are already airborne, or checking through customs, scouring phone books, hiring boats to take them quickly upriver. They will be packing satellite phones, PalmPilots, and GPSs, local dictionaries, Lonely Planet guides, open bank drafts, automatic pistols, Dexedrine, Visa cards, Kaopectate, Xanax, cocaine, letters of proprietary claim from NLog Communications, and cartons of Marlboros for purposes of barter. They will get where they are going but we will not be there. They will find instead these stories of where we have been and what we have seen.

In place of ourselves we offer the written documents that follow, partly out of simple respect for each agent's arduous journey, but with an intuition also about his or her misgivings, and with compassion for the many troublesome addictions that afflict the emissary sent on an errand of violence.

To these loyal marshals' distant master we concede this: we understand you mean us no good, that you are cunning, and that you have the support of many in our country who regard works of the imagination unreviewed by your committees as disruptions in the warm stream of what pleases them—product availability, job advancement, pretty scenery, buying a ticket that wins. We will not describe or attempt to defend the lives that may recently have brought each of us to your attention, being wary of what you will make of them in consultation with the national media. I have asked the other recipients of your letter instead to recall the moment in which they recognized the transformation that led to the work that so infuriated you—Lisa Meyer's installation *AdSpeak,* when it opened in Toronto; Susan Begay's mural of the terrorist Kit Carson's depredations at Canyon de Chelly; Eric Rutterman's translations of Tukano mythology and the play Emilio Chavez developed from them, which opened at the Mark Taper in Los Angeles; the private correspondence of Corazon Aquino edited by Jefferson deShay, which so embarrassed your predecessors.

Instead of a defense of the Republic, thrown in the corporate face of your governance, instead of another map to the kingdom of your frauds, an exposé of your pursuit of the voter as a mail-order customer, we give you a description of the events that changed us, that led to our decisions no longer to be silent, no longer to hunker down in the small rooms of our lives.

It is also our intention to break these stories out ahead of your avenging fist, to get them, through the agency of a sympathetic and defiant publisher, directly into the hands of men and women who stand at similar thresholds, before you stifle their initiative with your intimidations.

We regard ourselves as servants of memory. We will not be the servants of your progress. We seek a politics that goes beyond nation and race. We advocate for air and water without contamination, even if the contamination be called harmless or is to be placed there for our own good. We believe in the imagination and in the variety of its architectures, not in one plan for all, even if it is God's plan. We believe in the divinity of life, in all its human variety. We believe that everything can be remembered in time, that anyone may be redeemed, that no hierarchy is worth figuring out, that no flower or animal or body of water or star is common, that poetry is the key to a lock worth springing, that what is called for is not subjugation but genuflection.

We trace the line of our testament back beyond Agamemnon, past Ur, past the roots of the spoken to handprints blown on a wall. We cannot be done away with, any more than the history of the Sung dynasty can be done away with, traveling as it does as a beam of coherent light far beyond our ken. We cannot, finally, be imprisoned or killed, because we remember and speak.

We are not twelve or twenty but numerous as the motes of dust lining the early morning shafts of city light. We are unquenchable and stark in the same moment that we are ordinary. We incorporate damage and compassion, exaltation and weariness-to-the-bone.

These pages are our response to your intrusion, your order to be silent, your insistence that we have something to talk over.

> Owen Daniels, independent curator,
> author, *Commerce and Art in America,*
> on leaving Paris

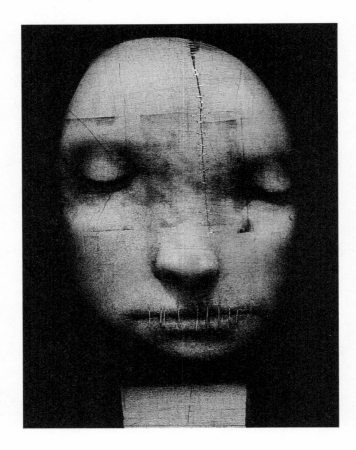

Río de la Plata

I watched my best efforts turn to coal. I would gaze west over the city at the end of the day and not be able to recall even the names of the colors in the sky. I had lost, long before this, the ability even to write a sentence that might break through. For twenty-two years I'd kept a journal, writing out each day what I believed, what I hated, what I desired. Sometimes I would make small drawings in the margins, not illustrations really, but other ways to say what I meant. When I could no longer find the words, these lines would still reflect my beliefs and emotions. When I could no longer even draw the line, I put the journals away.

My mother was a restaurateur. For many years she had a nice place on Avenida Alberdi in Flores, in the center of Buenos Aires. Many women who knew her revered, even envied her—suave, accomplished, vivacious. The restaurant was full every evening, and the food and service, extensions of her dedication and grace, were celebrated year after year in the local and international guides.

When I came home from school in New Haven, Connecticut, I would host for her and give the regular maître d' a few weeks off. At an early age, then, I began to appreciate the difference between sincerity and sycophancy, as people negotiated their reservations. I was able to separate those who wished only to be seen from those who admired the daring or intuition behind certain entrées on Mother's menus. I could easily spot the braggarts, distinguish them from those who could host a conversation about something other than their own ideas while they ate. With the regulars, I came to know their flaws as well as their tastes, and to appreciate their allegiance.

All this knowledge—about how people comport themselves around pleasure and indulgence, about social maneuvering and material expense—did me no good, however, when it came to my father. I didn't take in as deeply as I should have the evidence for deception. I was so caught up with social spectacle, I didn't perceive the transparency of life.

My father kept Sonia Bendales a secret from Mother and me for three or four years. Then, in one of those accidents fate likes to arrange, Sonia drove the Mercedes 500SL he'd given her into another woman's car on a busy corner of Calle

Rivadavia. The other driver, one Beatriz Orchada, shaken up but not really hurt, happened to be a mid-level manager in the accounting firm my father used for his many ventures. As part of her regular duties it fell to Beatriz to review the comptroller's report filed on the accident. Her indignation got away from her. In a few insouciant sentences it was declared that Beatriz had caused the accident. But it was Sonia who had run a red light. If Beatriz Orchada hadn't been making a right turn, Sonia might well have killed her.

The report ended with a request, that the purchase of an identical car for Ms. Bendales be arranged right away.

Beatriz went straight to my father and confronted him—a big miscalculation for all of us. She should have known to handle the matter discreetly through her own boss. Sitting there in his office, Beatriz quickly understood that it was just going to be swept under the rug, along with all the rest of the expense Beatriz knew about to accommodate Sonia's flamboyant personality. Beatriz phoned my mother anonymously and filled her ear. When Father came home that evening, he found Mother had packed his suitcases. Until he came to his senses, she said, he should live somewhere else.

Father was quick to make his decision. He divorced us, married Sonia, arranged an apartment for us nearer the restaurant, and moved Sonia into the only home I'd known since I was ten. Among other things, Mother and I lost the spectacular and consoling view across the Río de la Plata we'd had from the top floor of that building.

I was twenty-four. I had finished my degree and also gotten a license to practice architecture in Argentina. I might have stayed in the States, but during the time I hosted those evenings for Mother, I'd felt such promise for the future of Buenos Aires. I was also fairly well connected locally through my parents, and during my years in America I had honed a certain aggressiveness. By the time I was twenty-eight I was running my own firm, and before I was thirty I landed my first American commission, a monument to striking steelworkers killed at Homestead, Pennsylvania, in 1892. Between what I earned and what Mother made at the restaurant (Father still retained his part of the ownership), we lived comfortably.

I am a reasonably attractive woman. Men, however, hardly inquired, except for the one thing. Better with oneself, I would joke with Mother, than with such men. She told me it was my penchant for contempt, a streak of belligerence in me, that kept men at bay. I said she knew too little about independent women. She said I knew too much. I said I was educated about people's underhandedness and men resented my determination to do something about it. She shrugged. Then, often as not, the discussion would veer into a denunciation of my father, my mother's hands trembling occasionally at the memories.

After the divorce I viewed my life as a horse race. Whatever satisfaction I drew from my work—another commission, a prize, the growth of my billings, the expansion of my staff—I would match against what Sonia accomplished. She lived out in the open now, a kind of public farce which my father endured for reasons I will not get into. She had no work of her own, unless you would call the practice of insult work—her dramatic and indignant dismissals of whatever didn't please her, that laughable hauteur she affected, all of it lampooned anonymously in the gossip and society columns. Her politics, like her wardrobe and her taste in art, came directly from supermarket magazines.

Sonia was an actress, not a person. A client of mine has a phrase to denounce the nouveau riche of America: *un populacho empeñado en no educarse con un poder económico pasmoso,* "a willfully uneducated people with stupefying economic power." That was Sonia.

Well, it was a lot of time, years in fact, given over to reviling Sonia and competing with her, and despising my father and waiting for him to be impressed. I would tell myself that my fabulous life (as I saw it) was an intimidating vindication, a triumph of determination. I fed on hatred and kept a measure of it in every box of my life. I should have seen what was coming, a long, slow slide down an incline of bitterness, but I imagined I was well past all that. I would say to myself, I do not need the validation of any man, husband, lover, or father. I do not require any evidence of my father's love in order to receive another commission. I do not need for my father to be an honorable man in order to hold my head up at parties where I may encounter the two of them, her all dressed up like Marilyn Monroe, an idée fixe of my father's.

This was the life I lived—energetic, creative, financially successful, professionally admired—but it was not a life I could fully believe in. I wrote in my journal about the conflict, year after year, describing unspeakable and sometimes incomprehensible angers, yearnings I could not satisfy—and then in the mornings I would waltz into my office, an apparently confident woman I felt more and more apart from.

I willed myself to believe that my mother was strong enough to overcome the indignity of her betrayal, to let go her losses expeditiously, as if they were broken limbs pruned after a storm. Many people came to our apartment to offer her their support; more often, they went to the restaurant, under the impression, I suppose, that dining there more frequently would help. But when she did not revive the measure of gusto they expected, when she appeared too acquiescent, most of these women drifted away. The ones who kept up their prodding were the ones most bitter about their own lives, at a loss for a solution to their own particular hatreds. They smoked cigarettes with her in the kitchen while she worked up the day's menu, urging her toward some sort of revenge, variations on plots they all knew from the soaps, but which, they emphatically concurred, had been carried out too ineffectively.

She'd had grief enough. The day Sonia moved into our old apartment, she hired a janitorial service to clean it. In that rite of exorcism and purification, many of my mother's most cherished things were broken, dumped into a box, or simply thrown out. One afternoon, just before my mother arrived at the restaurant, Sonia showed up to claim the two most valuable paintings on the wall, cityscapes by Antonio López García. She donated them to a fund-raising effort for a new hospital in Palermo, the part of the city where she and my father lived.

And then one day I came home from work to find Mother in the living room with an envelope in her lap, and with the look of having been there in the blue wing chair for a long time. She was gazing out the front window into the pine trees growing in Parque Avellaneda, their crowns churning in the invigorating spring blow I had just come in out of. She extended the envelope without looking at me.

It was a handwritten note from her physician, sentences of comfort and encouragement which could not obliterate the two words: *Parkinson's disease.*

We arranged our lives to accommodate her loss of strength and mobility. Her sister's eldest daughter, a woman who ran a restaurant in another part of Buenos Aires called La Boca, a very competent and likable person, took over the restaurant. When I could no longer see to all of Mother's needs I brought in private care, a decision which made it disturbingly clear to me that, apart from her, I had nothing to hold my attention except my work.

I felt I'd arrived at a dead end. I was thirty-five. I had no prospect of children. I could not say that I knew anyone who had taken the trouble to know me—nor had I done that myself, so that now someone might give me a sympathetic ear. I'd lost track of my close friends from school. I didn't have the scaffolding of a religion to turn to. And I had not discovered anything in recent years to revitalize me—no book, no performance, no movie. I no longer even made the effort. In fact, I couldn't stand to read more than one or two stories in the papers anymore—it all seemed to be about adapting life to machinery, or scenarios for creating wealth, or politicians promising a future for us that had already come and gone. Worse, the news came festooned with ads, hounding the reader, imploring him to improve his looks, his appeal, his temperament, his prospects with one or another sort of purchase. The manic opportuning, page after page of it, every day, alternately depressed and infuriated me.

I did not resent my mother's illness, the burden of worry that she had become for me; but she began to stand out as part of an indictment I felt for leading a life that had become little more than an expression of irritation. Outside of my creative work, those actual hours of imagining and drawing a building or a monument against the restrictions of a set of specifications, I felt no relief from my anger. And then, finally, I could no longer manage to squeeze any satisfaction out of my work. I would pour myself into some high-minded, pro bono project only to discover that something crucial in me would not engage, and the project would fall apart like mercury spilled across a table.

I gave up trying to explain to myself what my anger was about. It was more than Sonia and my father, more than the empty-headed boosterism of the papers and the venal commerce of their advertising pages. It was rooted in a vast and seemingly intractable injustice that plagued the precincts of every city. I understood it better when I was young, because I simplified it; and I had long believed that my life stood in opposition to it all, that it was a renunciation. But I couldn't maintain this now. I felt increasingly detached from the principles that were supposed to be behind everything I did.

What had begun to weigh on me more than anything was the silence of everyone in the city, myself included. We moved from scandal to scandal—sexual, political, fiscal, environmental—with a shrug of the shoulders. Children killed themselves in the barrios and we turned the page. For reasons that ended with the Second World War or that had to do with national pride, I forget which, we attacked the British in the Malvinas. Businessmen cheated, powerful men could pay to circumvent any law, things fell apart that shouldn't—buildings, airplanes, human lives—and no one was to blame. Factories closed and men went down the drain.

There was no enemy, or the enemy lived in another country, or it was God's will.

One morning I opened a letter from the mayor of Buenos Aires, inviting me to discuss the design of a monument to the city's longshoremen. I called a friend, Deirdre Cantelaria, instead, and offered to sell her my business. It took five minutes. I went to the bank and set up funding to keep Mother and me in reasonable comfort. We moved from Flores to a smaller apartment in San Justo, way west in the city, and far from the river I had grown up next to. I was relieved initially, but I knew I was still running away. Images of the disjunction in my life pursued me like a dog that never tired. And it never lost my trail.

I offered my mother nothing but silence at our meals.

That same year, Sonia was diagnosed with pancreatic cancer. When she died Father asked us to move back in with him, in Palermo. Mother rolled her eyes when she read the letter.

We never considered it.

I tried to hide my deterioration from her, the loss of meaning which seemed like dry rot working its way deep into a house. I left the apartment purposefully every morning, moved briskly down the sidewalk, but had no intention, no aim beyond completing the most routine of errands. The fawning insincerity of people I met at the occasional party I still attended, the ubiquity of every kind of noise in the streets—jackhammers, radios, fights—the long rows of prescription drugs, hers and mine, in the bathroom, the attitude of entitlement with which perfect strangers would shove you aside at a counter were like a series of punches that gave me a headache every day. I was consumed with indignation at the least evidence of injustice. The smallest manifestations of privilege or prerogative incensed me. But no sense of not being implicated protected me.

Many an afternoon found me on a bench somewhere, looking back on my work as some sort of burlesque. I'd lost completely the distinction between what was true and what was false in my life.

On the worst days, I would make the long walk to the Río de la Plata and stare off across the river to the shores of Uruguay, hoping the expanse of that eternal water would give me hope. But on my return I would always find myself in the same narrow, dispiriting alley. When Mother died, I decided, I would just end it.

As her Parkinson's advanced, she was not always sure of her words, but she was quite sensitive to the subcurrents in our apartment, those rivers about which no one speaks because they fear the waters are too deep or that all will drown, once the dam is breached. Sometimes when I walked into her bedroom she would give me a sign that she was lucid, the movement of one finger or an almost comical look of self-awareness, amazement she was still alive.

One evening in 1985, after dinner, we were sitting together having our tea and she handed me a book. I turned it over in my hands, not knowing what to make of it, or of her gesture. It was Viktor Frankl's *Man's Search for Meaning*.

"You need to read this now," she said.

I gave her a sardonic smile. "Will it comfort me?"

"I met your father in Bergen-Belsen, fourteenth of July, 1943," she said. She did not pause for this revelation to sink in. "When you have read this, when you think you understand what it means, and not just in that analytic mind of yours, you ask your father to tell you how we came to be there. And then how we came to be in Brooklyn when you were born, and finally here in Buenos Aires. Ask him about all the things we were trying to escape."

I felt such a sense of shame before her. And she gave me such a look, the compassion only a parent can offer her self-absorbed child.

I began the book that evening stunned, which made it almost an act of distraction. But Frankl's description of his spiritual crisis in Auschwitz pulled me forcefully in and I read it straight through. His triumph over despair, his refusal to become the victim of his own sense of injustice, was mesmerizing. I scrawled questions in the margins. "Who is the family, waiting at home, for whom you choose life?" I wrote. "What comes after freedom from suffering?"

The next morning I dug out an old journal, the one I had last kept, and tried to write. I tried to get the tumble of emotions and thoughts I was experiencing to come together: my mother's revelation, which she may have chosen to make to me now because she knew she was dying. My strangely euphoric sense of renewal on finishing the book. The choices I might now make.

I knew I did not want to see my father, not right away. Instead, after writing out more of the flood that was pushing through me, crossing words out, rearranging sentences and paragraphs, I went to find Ernesto Guadalquivir. Ernesto and I had gone through architecture school together in the late sixties but had not spoken much since those days, now long past. Two or three times I'd been to openings at a print shop he owned in San Justo where he had broadsides and limited-edition books he'd published on display. He also had a small list of trade books, many of them about the culture of the Guaraní Indians. He was Marxist-Leninist when we first knew each other but, to judge from what he had published, his views had softened over time. He had apparently given up strident accusations for accommodation.

I wanted to share with Ernesto what I had written. For the first time since I had put away my journals I felt as if I had thrown off the fever of a jungle disease, that I was now able to make a coherent and even penetrating statement. My words were not punctuated with anger or built up on abstractions. They opened out onto possibilities that were strikingly new to me. I was not at all sure about the courses now possible, my thoughts still so compelled by Frankl's genius; but I felt I might realize again in conversation with Ernesto the beliefs and emotions of my early years, find a politics now that did not paralyze me with wrath, and that could lead to a statement as vital and unambiguous as the monument to the steelworkers at Homestead.

Like me, Ernesto understood how much thinking had to go into the design of a building that stood strong but lithe. It was the same process that once opened the walls of the French cathedrals to the passage of light. With the newly discovered flying buttress in place to take the weight of the roof, the once solid walls could frame expanses of glass. The dark caves of the eleventh century transformed into halls of light.

That morning, before going to visit Ernesto, I called Deirdre to see if she might give me some work, a project that would focus my initial efforts to turn this new clarity of purpose into solid dimensions. I looked in the papers for a studio. When I was back into a good rhythm, I decided, then I would go and see my father. I did not want to ask about Bergen-Belsen but to ask him instead to explain to me how love compels. And when he finished I would ask him to listen while I spoke. I wanted to articulate to him what I believed and

what I opposed. And then ask him to describe the
world he felt we were both caught up in. In that
way, as I imagined it, we might reach the shores of
Uruguay together.

> Lisa Meyer, installation artist,
> landscape architect, the Arabella
> Memorial, Minneapolis, the Damien
> Monument, Damascus, Jordan, on
> leaving La Plata, Argentina

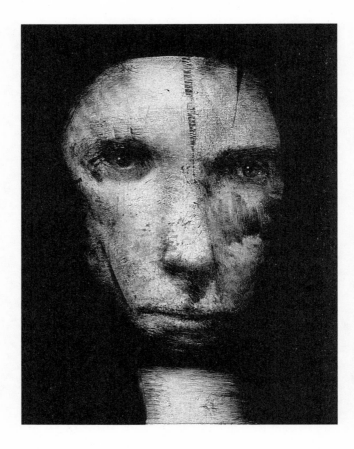

Mortise and Tenon

When I was five I was raped by a man who told me he was a doctor, that this was a treatment I needed. To deflect my mother's suspicion, he gave her money for rent and occasionally bought us a piece of furniture or gave Mother a physical, no charge. He took me into the backseat of his car on side roads or to his hovel of an apartment, year after year, and then my mother fell in love with a man who asked her to marry him. They moved far away from that place and took me with them. When I could bring myself to speak about it, her new husband told me that I would have to get over it, that the doctor had run a hospital, that he had done many good things. I needed to get past it, to get on with my own life.

With this instruction, then, I went ahead. I made it work. As I grew older I understood that some parts of me were inaccessible, frozen or asleep, but others weren't, and that by relying on these parts I could have a good life. I wasn't one to deny the brutality or insidiousness of what had happened—the painful sodomies, the fears of inadequacy around women, the early departure from home—but I perceived myself, accurately I thought, as a young man with only a slight limp, a defect few noticed and one that did not slow me down. As my working years began to accumulate—work in many different circumstances on four continents—and as I was confronted more often on the streets by the emaciated, the burned, the limbless, even the crucified once, the feelings of self-pity that I still harbored came to seem like cowardice. I was careful not to nurture them further when things went wrong. In those years I saw destitute fathers on their knees in the roads, begging of other men, who ignored them. I saw children, pawing in refuse for food and things to sell, beaten senseless by the police. I saw indentured prostitutes standing catatonic in their doorways, and the elephant men of the region on display for a small charge. In the light of these terrors, I came to see my own experience—the sudden flash images of choking, of being pummeled like a rag doll, rammed, and then thrown aside—as a kind of instruction. It was through the vividness of my own memories, I believed, that I could truly understand something of the lives of those for whom harm never slept.

I nursed no hatreds in those years, no desire for

revenge that I was aware of; but neither had I any true companion, nor any experience of life as I imagined it could be in a home—support given without judgment, food prepared as an act of love, the guardian silence, the kiss good-night. I made an itinerant's living as a finish carpenter and fine woodworker. I had good hands and a good eye, and a sense of proportion that made my designs widely acceptable. I moved between furnished room and furnished flat, first in my own country and then in the countries of other cultures, carrying my tools and making things I believed were beautiful: armoires, dining tables with matching chairs, sea chests, tansus with their many sliding doors and compartments. I worked in exchange for meals, a clean bed, some private space, and a few books, and for money enough to keep traveling, for gift giving, and for keeping up a reliable set of tools.

I was conscious of the emotions of love, so the necessary partings sometimes made me feel like a cracked vase, something from which the water had drained and in which the flowers had withered. It was a long while, of course, before I understood that my arduous efforts to be kind to each person, my expressions of compassion and acts of generosity, my will to accommodate were all a sort of mask. I could express love strongly, but I could not accept it, could not allow myself to be loved.

I could not, then, really claim to know love.

Once, on a train between Madras and Bangalore, I realized, watching feral dogs fight over food on a platform, that I regarded myself unconsciously as a pariah, beyond anyone's touch. My regular stints as a good neighbor one place and another, even the attractiveness of my work, the flawless cutting of a dovetail joint, were a wall behind which I dwelled. What I, in truth, feared were not the repeated departures from a well-made life, with the comfort of its routines, the loyal companionship, the sweet conversation over meals. I feared that a desire to stay on would overwhelm me, that I would not leave. My life would then include reciprocities I was not prepared for. I would have to fake the life unfolding in my blind spot.

To understand myself as a pariah, a person who chooses to be an outcast, was a relief. On disembarking in Bangalore that time, I was willing to concede that I was less than what I had imagined— a man with only a slight limp. The damage, I could say, had been more extensive. If I accepted myself in that moment as an outcast, a species of leper, it was not out of self-pity, however. It was out of humility, as I understand the word. I was going to play to exactly what I was. I would give up my hazy notions of someday living a different life, and fully embrace this life I had: useful, harmless, and chosen freely. I would now live as if I were even more fully the result of my own decisions.

On the walk from the train station to the home of my acquaintance, I realized I was making a new peace with my past. I had not gotten away as uninjured as I wanted to believe from the episodes in that shabby room; but considering the number of homes open to me, that I traveled without restraints, and that I possessed so many stories I could create a place for myself at nearly anyone's table, from Addis Ababa to Christchurch, I had not paid too high a price.

My friend Gileathal opened the door at my knock that night, pulled me through the opening with an embrace, introduced me to his four children, then to his wife and her brother, and we sat down right away to eat. Gileathal related to the others the circumstances of our first meeting, exaggerating it all to encourage laughter; and I of course embellished his version. The evening then grew quieter and I entertained Belinda, Gileathal's youngest daughter, with cat's cradle tricks. I tied her a string loop of her own and taught her how to make "the fish" and "the wagon."

Gileathal sent one of his sons to the station after my bags and tools and then showed me to quarters at the back of his house. I stretched out full length on the narrow straw tick mattress, satisfied and pleasantly exhausted. I felt, after my insight on the train, more honestly engaged with my life now. I was just at the edge of sleep when Belinda came into the room. She walked directly to the bedside. Our eyes met, hers gleaming dark in the rays of an alley lamp slanting through the window. She took my face in her hands and kissed my forehead, then walked from the room.

The sound of the door latch closing, the bolt sliding slowly up the striker plate until it clicked shut, expanded the volume of space in the room and created a kind of vacuum into which I silently tumbled. I fell through memories that appeared to have no common thread. The impression of Belinda's kiss was as vibrant on my skin as a clapper's strike on a bell wall, and in the harmonics of it I lost my composure. I pulled my knees up to my chest and tried to hold my breath. What a laugh! The humble pariah. The courteous itinerant, the carpenter and cogitator Ishmael! I lay there staring at the expanse of my ache, the size of my anger.

In the morning I went off with Gileathal to his cabinet shop. He was kind enough to introduce me to his workers as someone who could teach them enough about joinery, about hiding feather blocks in miters and about customizing lap joints (to hold even the softest woods together) that they would be able to eliminate, even more than they already had, a reliance on nails, screws, and other metal fasteners. I had a gift, he said, for imagining a tight and lasting joint.

For my part, I eagerly took in Gileathal's instruction on the character of local woods, lumbers I'd never handled before, and we discussed which job orders I might take on. Clients came in. Gileathal introduced each one around. When we took breaks for tea I began to get acquainted with the other men, in the banter of politics and neighborhood news. I felt that morning, however, the urgency of an errand I couldn't define. Perhaps it was only the need of a few hours to myself after my rough night. As he was closing the shop that evening, I told Gileathal I was going to explore this quarter of the city further before coming home, and asked him to recommend a restaurant.

The city unfolded around me, all seemingly haphazard and percolating, houses with intricate chalk designs on the stoops, rug stalls, two men in a courtyard playing the veena and nagara, the smell of wood smoke and spiced food. I was not surprised when the proprietor of the restaurant I chose figured me easily for who I was. My waiter presented me with a local beer, a good one, and it was his treat. The food was excellent and I felt refreshed. When I paid the bill I thanked each person individually and stepped outside, more or less certain of the route back.

I lit a beedi and made my way up the street.

I did not feel the cut across my hand or notice the convergence of shadows until a blow to my sternum sent me backward through a doorway.

"Hello. Hey, hello!" said a man poking me in the chest with a knife, a staccato pinprick.

"What the hell," I mumbled. "What is this?"

No answer. A match flared and a small boy lit a candle. There were three others, the one with the little knife taller, clearly their leader.

"We don't have to talk to people like you," this boy said, "but we can kill you right now, you white bastard, how about that? Would you like that?" His pupils were weirdly dilated in the flickering light. He wore bell-bottom trousers and a windbreaker with a torn zipper, and he began to deliver a melodramatic screed I'd heard many times from street toughs, in good English. I didn't sense in the three smaller boys the resolve to do serious harm, let alone kill me. On the dirt floor at my heels I saw part of a broken chair. There would be no reasoning with the tall boy, but I could land one blow and run. The door to the street had been shut but had no lock.

It was only as I flexed against the insistent and now bounding pain in my right hand that I realized the tendon over the thumb had been cut. I had no grip. The tall boy sketched the air in front of me with the knife, in a singsong way, seething with indignation. He offered a religious rationale for his indictment of my culture. Transfixed, his friends studied him, then me. The cat, the mouse.

"Listen to me!" I interrupted. "Listen to me now. I can take you to the place you want." I had no idea where I was going, but the boy stopped ranting. "What you hate, I hate," I continued. "Yes! You see? And I can unlock the gate that keeps you out, and let you in. Yes, I can. And then what? You'll have it just as you want. And then every-one—your story will be big, everywhere."

The boys listened closely. The tall one took a step toward me as I pretended to sit down, to demonstrate I was prepared to talk this out, to make my meaning clearer. I moved the chair leg out of the way with my left hand and came up with it, swinging full into the boy's head. The wallop turned the boys' faces as one, like birds on a wire. The little scimitar knife went flying. The lanky boy spun against the wall, his tongue lolling, his eyes gone half white as he slid to the floor. Complete stillness; then one of the smaller boys scrambled after the knife and I went down with the other two punching me in a struggle for the chair leg. I burst to my feet with it, throwing them off with a roar that staggered the room. "Nooo! Nooo!" I bellowed. I drove the three of them backward with the leg, lashing at them in a fury, knocking the knife into the air.

"You little shits," I screamed. "Never, goddamn you, *ever* touch me!"

The stunned boy on the floor was turning slowly onto his knees, groping to raise himself. "Nooo!" I bawled, and charged. I swung as hard as I could left-handed, straight up into his face. He pitched up, dropped, and was still.

I flung the chair leg in front of the other boys. They stood aghast, as if there had been a complete misunderstanding.

"Get this guy to a doctor," I said, disgusted now with them all.

They didn't move.

"He's sick. He's very sick," I said. "Do you understand? He needs a doctor."

They stepped around me and began to look after him.

I took the few steps to the door and went out. My trousers were sopping with blood, my shirt the same. I could feel the onset of delirium, the tremors of acid fury coming, the desire for revenge ballooning. I could not keep my attention focused on the pattern of the streets, but went with what pieces I recognized and eventually found the restaurant. They walked me to a hospital and called Gileathal. A night doctor sewed the tendon together. She had a knowing and amused look, an ironic manner, perhaps from having read in my face the fear of what it would mean to a man like me to lose a thumb.

The sense of injustice over what had occurred and the urge for vengeance had by now intensified, though what I most wished for just then was sleep. I talked it through with Gileathal. He said the hospital had called the police, and that they had caught the boys. Tomorrow they would come around to the shop. Gileathal's attitude seemed to be that cruelty simply abides, wickedness always festers, despite our efforts. We are only fooling ourselves, trying to be rid of these infections. He speculated that the older boy had just gone too far—with drugs, with an act of daring, possibly with the excitement of the many frustrations he felt. Families today, he said, are no longer able to keep such a person in check. Too many of them burst in the street now, a pomegranate thrown in a fire.

The police will have a talk with the boy, Gileathal explained, get some idea of who he is, what his family situation is. Then they will find a place for him until they determine what to do. It could be that jail is the right place, so then there would have to be a trial. But perhaps some other course will be found.

"You're right," Gileathal said to me, "he's sick.

49

And it's the sickness we must treat. Once you have experienced such insults and wounds," he warned, gesturing at my hand, "if you're not careful, your original position here—to condemn him—will become your only position."

I fell in easily with his thoughts.

The thumb healed up well enough after a couple of months. "Aiyee," Gileathal would occasionally exclaim in mock despair over the quality of my finish work in the shop. "Let us hope he'll one day be a skilled cabinetmaker again, not a fellow continuing to borrow against our impeccable reputation here."

The older boy was a short time in prison and afterward went to see a healer. One morning he pulled up to the shop with a load of salvaged teak boards on a motorcycle truck. He unloaded it wordlessly and putt-putted away.

Something I never discussed with Gileathal afterward was how in those months after the incident I was able to reduce the height of the protective wall I had always kept around myself. I can only understand it this way: a fear of never fitting in, which I had carried all my life but which I had not been aware of, began to dry up. In its place came a sense that I had finished with something. When Belinda hugged me at night, I didn't any

longer move quickly to free myself from her
embrace. I no longer made light of her impulse.

When I went over these changes in myself, lying
in bed at night, I would sometimes recall a woman
named Kauko Hirai. She lived near Abashiri in
northern Hokkaido. Like her father, a university
professor there, she had never married. For many
years she had run a commercial nursery on several
hectares of land they owned together. In the past
we had enjoyed each other's company with more
than ordinary intensity. She was a discerning col-
lector of folktales, especially among the Ainu, the
traditional people of Hokkaido, nearly wiped out
by militant Japanese during the Meiji Restoration
in the nineteenth century. It was from her that I
first learned of the ability of a brown bear, their
eper, the dominant animal in Ainu culture, to heal
itself. I had long held on to this image, a bear
choosing among many small roots the one that
would promote the healing of a wound.

I had to tell Belinda the story one day.

I wrote Kauko. She wrote back immediately to
say that, yes, there was some work for me to do at
their home and to please come if I could. Also,
another old friend of ours, Naoki Kurasama, had
developed some problems that were forcing him to
close his furniture shop. Maybe I could talk with
him about the shop, she wrote.

So in 1982 I got ready to leave again, to say

good-bye at the age of thirty-six to Gileathal and his family and fly to Delhi, and then on to Narita, where I would take the train to Haneda and catch a flight to Abashiri. It was a risk, to consider making a home in Japan, but less than many I'd taken. And what I was now able to put to work, I had not possessed before.

> Gary Sinclair, cabinetmaker, land activist, editor, *Indigenous Culture: An International Journal of Folklore,* on leaving Kitami, Hokkaido

Traveling with Bo Ling

Innocence is a theme of mine. I could begin with Vietnam, myself, though you might well have in mind another place. The scene: rape, pillage, murder, torture, and humiliation beyond anybody's law. A theater of depravity, hypocrisy, self-delusion, and violent compulsions of every sort. I learned two things in Vietnam: suffer harm, take risks, even commit murder to protect the people around you. Let the reporters elucidate the meaning of "freedom" back home in the slo-mo heartland. Let them parse *democracy* over cracked crab and a good Chardonnay. And I learned this: police your own people. If you don't, what they do, or attempt to do, will harm or diminish you all.

No one is around to see, understand, and a man swerves to hit a dog. The dog lies dead in the road. If the dog were a problem, say an old girlfriend, the problem would be over. On another day the man swerves toward another dog, but he must chase after this one a little, running up over the sidewalk to get it. A witness, a man his age, gives him a sly smile. Is it out of envy? Is it out of admiration, out of fear? The man has a meaning now, a mission: to hunt down dogs.

He wonders why they run.

Many who lost their innocence in Vietnam didn't want to. They thought they did, until they got up close. The loss of innocence, in such killing fields as I saw, was compelled. It could not be avoided. This is not the same as making an informed decision to step into mayhem, or simply stumbling into carnage, once, unprepared. The sudden hum in the spine and scrotum, the turgidness of the forebrain, the looseness of the bowels that come with such exposure are, for some, not warning enough. The loss of innocence becomes an appetite to experience the loss again. For others, being suddenly stripped, the collapse of the façade of one's gentility, brings with it a peculiar feeling of debt, and the maddeningly elliptical question of who pays for someone else's loss of innocence.

Or consider a loss of sexual innocence, whether by force or choice. Remembered as a loss, it can contribute to a life of grief, a life of anger or numbness. What comes of the choice to no longer be innocent is different for every pilgrim; but to choose is to risk a region of the soul.

Here is an anomaly: a man pausing to reload a

weapon glances sideways into a room where another man in his platoon is raping a girl. He holds her up with one hand against a wall by her throat. The witness may feel indelibly stained. The moral combustion may direct his fury into some defilement of his own. Or the scene may end forever his curiosity, his taste, for inflicting harm. Or consider this: during dinner a young woman decides she will make love for the first time, with this boy sitting across from her. He, too, is innocent, their sex is clumsy, and the union lasts a lifetime. Or his sex is mechanical, sophisticated, and when he departs he is gone forever. He leaves her with something she won't forget.

Until our final day, no matter how adventuresome, we are destined to remain innocent of experience—innocent of certain musics and exotic dishes, this or that climate, of the sensation of parachuting from a plane or breathing underwater from a tank of air. I mean innocent here, not ignorant. Ignorance suggests a cut of willfulness. Innocence implies lack of opportunity. The bigot is ignorant. The man in remotest Congo who has never seen a white is conceivably innocent of the white race.

We didn't know what we were getting into in Vietnam; the innocent as well as the ignorant came home wounded. And we've been trained to the belief that innocence can never be recovered. You can't not have murdered if you have. You can't choose not to have seen what you regret, not to have been aroused by what you later condemned.

Who is the enemy? we fully trained soldiers asked ourselves in Vietnam. The corrupt Diem family? Francophobes among the Chinese? The lieutenant's West Point professors? The phatic orators in Congress? The corporate carney men? Us? An argument no one ever settled. The question itself was a luxury, a needling distraction. Five minutes before he stepped out of an armored personnel carrier and took a rocket-propelled grenade through his abdomen, a corporal in my platoon said, "Evil—it's in the DNA, man. We dig it." As witness, perpetrator, and victim, he was then complete in his knowledge of death. And my innocence, of what it meant to become a blind man by virtue of those very same fragments, a man without a scrotum or a penis, ended. In the flash oven of the APC behind me, the other six were incinerated.

When I returned from Vietnam, my father told me I was now no longer ignorant (he meant innocent) of the world, the world of real politics, of the ideology and economic investment that compel war, as it had been personally inflected for me at Dak Phong Lu, a three-minute firefight that left forty-six of seventy alive, some barely, after a volcano of light and heat so unremitting glass dripped from the vehicles like syrup and of some of us nothing was found.

He was sorry for all that had happened. I could have told him that some of what I had learned, certain twists of logic and desire within human nature about which I was no longer uninformed, I did not actually have to experience in order to imagine. Isn't this one reason, I wanted to say, why men wrote war books, *Paco's Story*, *Dispatches*, *The Things They Carried*, *A Rumor of War*? Must each man kill in order to truly abjure the killing? Did men have to brutalize in order to understand the capacity?

It would have been cruel to confront him, a veteran of Omaha Beach and St.-Lô. I asked, "What *is* the lesson of war, Dad?" He said to be vigilant.

After a period of adjustment, a time of confusing and turbid bitterness, during which I made a nuisance of myself at social gatherings by drawing in innocent people—innocent of war, unaware of my intentions—with a recital of my grievances, seducing them through the pity they felt for me, then bombarding them with an annotated list of the murderous regimes our country has always supported, because their economies were good for American business, after those years of violence and fury, of serving the human compulsion to blame, I gave up attacking the innocent. (I couldn't abide the ignorant from the beginning.) After twelve years of this, with much help—the best of the therapists, no surprise, was another vet—I edged myself out into the pool of life again. My own loss of innocence had kept me a prisoner of my wounds during those years. By opening the door and walking out of that room, I regained a measure of that same innocence.

Twenty-two years after I came home from the war I married a North Vietnamese woman. She, too, was blind. We met in Santa Cruz, California, the town I'd grown up in and where she'd lived with the man who brought her there, who blinded her with lye for looking at another man. Few who pitied—or lamented—our circumstances knew I had not the means to help make a child, nor that there were many nights when we barely got ourselves across the minefields of each other's bitterness and rage. The latter was too private for us to reveal, the former a crude bulwark of our dark humor.

It was Bo Ling who suggested, after we had been married two years and gotten a small house north of Santa Cruz, near Pigeon Point, that we go back to Vietnam.

We flew to Ho Chi Minh and then up to Da Nang, Tourane to the French. From there someone drove us up to Hué, then through Quang Tri, the country of my other baptism. Another fifty miles up the coast was Long Dai, a small city on a river where once Bo Ling had lived and where, in fact, I had killed some people.

We tilted our heads back in the rush of air passing over the open car as we drove, like dogs ranging with keen noses, our hands brushing over each other's and clasping as we took in the countryside life we had known so differently. For each of us, sightless, the experience was like not quite being there but moving instead through a vivid recollection. What was lost on us, the shape and color of the fields, the hesitant wave of a stranger, was a gentle reminder of the fallibility of even the most earnest memory.

Despite our impairment, we got on all right. With infinite patience, Bo Ling's mother, Xuân Nhung, managed to keep us both on the road as she led us from place to place on our large-wheeled tricycles, to visit friends, to describe for us, to let us recall. The smells of the jungle, the acrid odor of wood smoke, the distant bell clang of water buffalo, the sputter of small motorbikes, the febrile heat brought back to me first the place and not my bravado, not the tang of gore, the local labyrinth of corruption, our hopeless pursuit of victory. That once-upon-a-time gumbo of piss-fury and grief, though, of shitting fear in the Vietcong tunnels, was never far off. And a recollection of the fantasies of torture and humiliation we concocted, which we swapped with other grunts and did try to practice, settled over me in the dark on the floor mats like a night sweat.

I did not feel regret over the killing. Even as I got to know Bo Ling's family, her brothers and their children, their neighbors around Long Dai, I regretted nothing. I felt instead some kind of affliction. I felt desolated. It was the desolation men who are drawn to sleek weapons and crisp uniforms feel, when they spill themselves for a cause not theirs, in that last ticking moment alone in Everyman's no-man's-land. During those days I'd tremble with the lessons of my innocence recalled, the years I'd given up, like a heroin addict, nursing the anger. Bo Ling's acceptance was an embayment. My face could not get enough of her body. I could not get enough of our silence together.

We were there a month. As she served me so I understood I served her complex and nearly inscrutable recriminations. We came home washed of the whole thing, having redeemed the insult of our wounds.

We were comfortable in that house near Pigeon Point. But after the trip to Vietnam, cobbling one thing and another together—we were living on my veterans' benefits, her alimony, and what the U.S. Navy was ordered to send of her former husband's benefits—Bo Ling and I wanted to finance trips to the Caribbean and to Greece, places where we could depend on the experience of sunshine spilling over us. We continued to lose our innocence on these journeys—the innocence of the overprotected child—trying foods we could taste but not see, searching for music that got inside us so much we'd gyrate together in the privacy of our hotel room. We were working on the long pattern of our life, drawing out what lay buried deep in each other, things that wouldn't have emerged, we believed, unless they expected to survive.

We heard a story on the radio one night in Morocco, about a blind man who had made himself a world authority on seashells. He did not need to know the color or the pattern. By touch alone, an intricate palpation, he separated one species of conch from another, each limpet, each cowrie, each chambered nautilus from its close relatives. An authority like that, I said to Bo Ling, that would become my goal.

With an intensity I was not capable of before marrying Bo Ling, I concentrated on the education of my fingers. I quickly chose a Japanese art, something that got my attention once in Kyoto, folding paper into the forms of animals and flowers. Origami. As I developed the dexterity that would lead to precision, and refined my touch so I could distinguish grain in my papers, I took an almost sexual pleasure in the work. The levels of perfection

63

I was able to achieve, on occasion, were all I needed to once again feel comfortable in the world. I knew some people bought my creations solely because of the transcendent smile I could now produce without effort, which they saw in a burned-over face with no eyes.

Darkness none of us wishes to know well, just enough to make us wary, alert, educated. It's light we want, the metaphor for God, as many would have it. The difficulty for me and Bo Ling as we worked, as we talked through our daily lives— making meals, making love—was that at the outset, in seeking an end to innocence, in deliberately seeking a certain measure of knowledge in foreign cities, one has no assurances. Will this be an encounter with darkness or the light, or something in between? Fearful of the dark, we might choose to stay innocent—to our detriment sometimes, sometimes to our benefit.

In my world of folded papers, which became as elaborate for me as childhood interpretations of the Bible, in Bo Ling's gentle companionship, and in what sometimes felt like a life of trysts for the two of us as we flew to Dakar, to Istanbul, to Cairns, I understood that I had found the finished design of a postwar life, the sleep free of nightmare.

. . .

Nearly every day now, it seems, I hear on the radio the protestations of businessmen who have been exposed, tobacco and chemical executives, bankers and corporate tallymen. "We did not know!" they declare. "Had we only known!" they exclaim. "We were misled by others," they testify, "and are ourselves the true victims of this breakdown in communications."

They arrogate an innocence few can believe they possess, and the gutted victims of their plots and fiascos—financial, military, social—spiral into oblivion. How many times in one's life, I would shout at Bo Ling, can a man claim innocence? Can a nation get away with saying "We had no idea how bad things were. Let us punish those responsible, and so preserve the innocent"? What depth of experience with evil does it take, I would demand, how much of the world's history of goons needs to be taken in, before a person ceases to participate?

I can still, you see, be yanked into a gyre, circling back to the war, to the core of deception that lay at its heart. I can grasp this much: it has ever been this way, from the invasions of Macedonia forty centuries ago by Anatolians to the Wehrmacht's blitzkrieg across Poland. Deceit, hypocrisy, self-delusion, breast-beating, greedy designs, the forbidden pleasure of violence running through wars that were sanctioned and ones that were not.

Wars without beginnings, wars with pauses but without ends.

War is an appetite. It is its own reason for being.

Unfortunately, with every war the dead must come, the maimed, the deranged, the frustrated, the guilt ridden, all those for whom war's champions, its believers, even its grateful survivors have no adequate answer. What is the question to which I am the answer, a blind eunuch with a face of melted wax?

How often, I ask myself, do these memories snare me? How hard do I go down? How long before I get up? Most of the bile is gone now. With Bo Ling, with my sheets of folded paper—here, young lady, a chrysanthemum and a tiger—I circle back less and less. I cannot undo the past, but I can make a present that will diminish its size, see to it that my experience of darkness does not take up more room than its due. My goal is no longer to ensure that the names of those who sent me to die are not forgotten, but to reach a place where I can recall their names only with difficulty.

Bo Ling has a plan to help us both. She wants to raise a child. She thinks we can adopt. I'm not strongly behind her on this, but she says this is because I cannot let go of enough of my anger. She may have something. Another goal, then: the loss of enough anger to become a father.

In my own terms—accepting the risk that

comes with a loss of innocence, not knowing whether you are preparing yourself for darkness or for the realm of light—for *me* to choose parenthood has some heft. It will be loaded with consequence. But not to follow it out, not to take the risk, wouldn't that finally leave you an isolate, your own grim island? Further, I tell myself, wouldn't love, the plunge with the greatest risk of all, fall short of its final loss of innocence if it did not take this step, if I never said to a small child, I give you my life?

It's this sort of thinking that makes me believe one day I will turn the putative tragedy of the world inside out. Having killed others, including a child, and been maimed, I might now raise a child I would never ask to compensate me for what I cannot resolve. I might love the child freely, asking no more from him—or her—than that he become highly discerning about the loss of the great pool of innocence with which he was born.

I would be vigilant, as once my father urged.

The wages of trauma, as I have written it out in my life, is anger. The resolution of that anger, say the therapists, breaks the grip of the traumatic event. But to resolve the anger—and this I got on my own—it's necessary to love. It's not enough just to arrive at a place where no one, not even yourself, is to blame.

You have to go further.

For several years now Bo Ling, from her own perspective, has also been telling me this. To wash out the anger, she says, fall in love. Be in love with a peach, she says, its summer juice running down your bare chest. Be in love with the sound of your brother's truck as it pulls up to the curb on a summer night with supper just ready on the table. Be in love with me, she says, when my fingers move slowly across her small belly.

Reengage your innocence here, in the Dresden of my face, she says.

> Harvey Fleming, Bravo Company, Second Battalion, 27th Infantry, military historian, author, *Incident at Kabul,* on leaving Tangiers

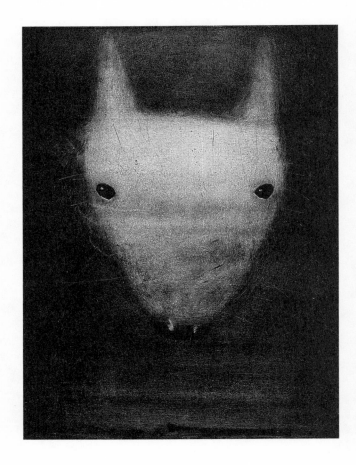

The Bear in the Road

Virgil brought two mugs of black coffee to the table along with some fry bread. We ate without talking and watched dayrise through frost-rimmed glass in the double-hung window. Boys had broken out the lower pane that past summer with a baseball. Virgil had taped clear plastic over the triangular shards, enough of a fix until he had time and money to get a new pane of glass. We could not see the ground clearly from the table, only the sky through the upper half of the window.

"Hear them coyotes last night?" I asked.

"Mmm."

"Wonder if they're after that little bear cub."

We'd seen a lone black bear cub the day before, out riding together. Virgil had marked it. He'd taken an intense interest in it.

"I'm going over to see Charlie Good Swan," he said, "about those calves. You can come along."

"I'd rather borrow a horse, if that's all right. I

71

want to go up Medicine Shield Creek, see if I can find that little bear."

"That's a good idea. Take that buckskin."

Virgil ate his bread and gazed up at the sky, where clear-weather cumulus were moving east on a high wind.

"All right, I'll go see Charles, and I'll see you back here later."

He went out to his truck and left.

I saddled the buckskin and rode away south, toward the escarpment where we'd seen the cub. I located our day-old tracks and began to range in the direction the bear had gone, looping back and forth looking for sign.

Whenever I studied the country around Virgil's like this, searching hard for something or hopeful of some opening, I'd feel the mind's language, the naming and analyzing of detail, slipping away from me. I'd feel again the wordless kinship I'd known with Virgil in my boyhood. It was an elusive and elevated physical sense of being present in the world. It chagrined me now, later in life, that I did not act on it then, that I was content to remain an observer despite the repeated invitation this sensation offered.

I looked close for the bear for a few hours. I found no trace of him, nor coyotes either, for that matter, and rode directly back in an opposite frame

of mind, with thoughts of another life pressing in
on me.

What strained at me about the state of the land
I was riding through, if I allowed the thought to get
in, was how it had emptied out. I never rode here
with Virgil as a boy that we didn't come on big
herds of antelope. I hadn't seen herds like that in
fifteen years. The same was true for the other animals. Fewer fox, jackrabbit, badger, golden eagle. It
was as though somehow they'd been sifted out
without anything else being disturbed. All you saw
anymore, really, were deer. Trophy hunting and
varmint hunting is what did it, I believe. Poisoned
baits, cattle ranching, fences. Thrill killing, whatever it is boys call it these days. Maybe once on a
day's ride now you saw a fox.

Virgil Night Crow met my mother in the thirties when she was a child growing up outside Glas-
gow, Montana. If she hadn't been a girl, my
grandparents probably would have let her run off
with Virgil's people, at least for a while. As it was
they just put up with the fascination she took with
them—and let Virgil know there was something
not altogether right about his interest in their
daughter, twenty years younger than he was. Virgil,
I'm certain, was polite and reassuring, and finally
paid them no mind. He'd locked onto something.

What he concentrated on, Mother said, was

teaching her detail and association in the country they traveled over, how one small thing signaled another. It had once all been his people's alone, south to the villages of the Mandan and Hidatsa on the Missouri, east to the Ojibwe country, north to where the Plains Cree were, west to the Gros Ventre, and southwest to the Crow. Assiniboine, Virgil's people were called, Stony to some. Mother said he knew that country, twig and dirt, the way she knew me: what it liked and didn't like and how all its known parts—the colors of the sky or chinook winds coming east to cross up a hard winter—could never together explain the mystery of what it was.

The country was broad and open to the Assiniboine, reeling plains of short grass and river breaks, wrinkling here and there into low hills and buttes. Buffalo country. When western Canada and the Louisiana Purchase were laid out, the dividing line ran straight through Assiniboine country.

"You could choose Canada or the U.S.," Virgil said one time. I'd been trying to get him to talk about how it felt, being closed in on a reservation. "George III or Thomas Jefferson, you could take your pick."

"You could?" I said, taken aback by the point in law but buying it anyway.

"Yeah," he deadpanned, "some of us are still working on it."

74

Virgil's way with broken treaties, land grabs, assimilation, and the rest was to move on, regardless, like the big prairie rivers in spring melt, the Milk or the Poplar, a quiet, heavy flow, nearly out of sight beneath the cutbanks.

He treated designing whites like a series of bad storms he had to weather.

When I was born he took me into his life as though I were a grandson, a relationship my father was never easy with. Still, summers I got to stay with Virgil. We'd ride up into Canada together. He taught me to hunt. Over the years, I got to know most everyone on the Fort Peck Reservation.

Virgil's place was on upper Porcupine Creek around Larslan. We lived off the reservation near Four Buttes, about forty miles away. My father moved us down to Wolf Point when I was about ten, when he quit ranching and went into real estate. I was back east at college when he moved everyone south to Miles City. My mother was killed there a couple of years later, a freak accident in a horse chute. My father was seeing another woman at the time. The first thing he did was clear the house of all the books my mother had bought and read, books she had impressed on me when I was young, and which had been for me a refuge from my father's scorn for ideas.

My brothers and sisters later moved out of state. My father married the woman. He now lives with one of her children in Cheyenne. When Virgil asked if they could bury Mother in those hills up around him my father said no.

Wherever I went with Virgil, he would teach me about concrete and practical things—finding water, tracking animals, which cactus fruits were okay to eat. He never ignored my questions or made me feel embarrassed. When I was fifteen, Virgil rode us up north of where Willow Creek comes into Porcupine Creek and left me there alone for four days to fast and dream, to find out who I was and what I was to do. I was eager for a vision and tried hard to find my way inside all that Virgil had told me about, describing the country right in front of me where animals moved around like people, walking up to you like they had something to say. But that whole time fasting I just felt scared and dumb. No vision came.

After law school I moved back to Havre and began to practice. I handled mostly treaty cases from the Fort Belknap, Rocky Boy, and Fort Peck reservations. It was what I believed in. Sometimes I'd go over and spend a week with Virgil. He was in his seventies by then. I'd always feel around him that our business wasn't finished.

Driving the Hi-Line back to Havre from Virgil's one night, I ran off the road trying to miss a bear. I

got out of the pickup, stuck pretty good in the borrow ditch but no great damage, and climbed back
up to the highway. I'd pumped a rifle cartridge into
the chamber of my old Colt .38-40, a slug that
would knock a horse sideways. I saw the bear two
hundred feet away, still standing the same place on
the two-lane macadam, a shadow in the lesser darkness with his shoulders against the sky. No one in
fifty years, I guessed, had seen a plains grizzly in
northeastern Montana.

The bear did not move but faded, it and the
night becoming one darkness.

I was twenty-six then. Two years later another
bear—Virgil looked over the claw marks and said
this, too, was a grizzly—tore the front screen door
off my place. I didn't want to get into it with Virgil
just then, about why a bear would do this, just tear
the door off and leave, but I was about to get married and anxious that Jill would now be living there
with me.

I had to have an explanation from him. Virgil
just shrugged. How was he to know?

The first fall we were married I took Jill up to
Lake Thibadeau for a few days. We watched ducks
and geese staging for migration, bald eagles hunting the stragglers. She liked hearing the red-winged
blackbirds and meadowlarks in the afternoon,
those fat, bright songs. Brewer's sparrows. We'd set
our tent up on the sandy doab of an old river bar.

The last morning, we got up to find fresh grizzly tracks all around. I tried to follow the bear's trail but lost it in shallow water in both directions.

When we got home I dropped Jill off and continued on alone another 218 miles to see Virgil. He didn't have a phone.

"He's trying to get your attention, I guess," Virgil said.

"What do you think I should do?"

"Pay attention."

"Jill is three months pregnant, Virgil, I can't be taking any chances here," I said.

He looked at me the way you might someone who repeatedly draws the wrong conclusions.

"Why don't you come over again next week," he said. "We'll go back to that place up on the Porcupine, where I took you when you were a boy. We'll look around."

He was telling me, so I just gave him a nod, okay.

I had a hard time getting away. I was in court in Helena most of the week, working on a case for the Gros Ventre, arguing with ranchers who believed in a God-given right to go after a stock-killing bear, even on reservation land, and who were relentless in expressing their beliefs about the Christian foundations of our country and other assumptions which they held to be trustworthy guides to right living.

I got to Virgil's late on a Friday night and found him already asleep. The next morning when he woke me it was still dark. We drove the highway north. Above where Porcupine Creek crosses a dirt road we got the horses out, the buckskin for me and a blue roan mare, and then rode some miles farther north to where a mixed stand of cottonwoods and box elder stood on a river bar. It was understood Virgil would wait for me there, just as he had twenty years before.

We both knew what this was about.

I continued up the dry streambed toward my old campsite, packing a blanket, a tarp, a jacket, and a couple bottles of water. Virgil had not been explicit, but I knew I was to attempt again to get a vision, the image of responsibility essential, in his view, to the leading of any kind of meaningful life. The intrusion of the bear, the bear's almost human insistence, was not lost on me; but I felt no burning need to rearrange my life to accommodate the bear. What I wanted was an explanation, a direction to head.

It was still early when I set off up the coulee. At a place where the high bank had collapsed, I saw, not so far away, a herd of pronghorn grazing. Skittish as they are, they paid me no mind, no more attention than they'd have given a flock of birds.

79

There were about a hundred of them, and I sat the horse awhile watching while they drifted the plain, the calves hieing up alongside their mothers whenever something in the wind or grass spooked them. Later I rode up on a badger, her new den obvious on a point bar with fresh dirt dark where she'd been digging. Like the pronghorn, she showed no alarm, but fixed me directly in her stare. About fifty feet away a coyote stood in the brush. When I reined in to see better what was up, the coyote gave me a look. It raised hairs in the runnel of my spine.

These signs made me more alert and hopeful. When I reached the head of the draw, I got off the horse and sat the ground awhile with the reins in my hand. None of the country around was familiar from the earlier time, though it had a freshness to it you didn't see farther south.

I picketed the horse and waited out the late afternoon light with some expectation—and fear, should the bear show up. When dark filled out the last unshadowed ground, I went to sleep on boughs of sagebrush I'd cut and worked into a mat.

I awoke with no memory of dreaming, but with a heavy feeling of being in empty and unfamiliar rooms. I was hungry, though not yet light-headed. Right away I saw the horse had pulled his picket. From the drag marks, I saw he'd headed back down the coulee to where Virgil was camped. It was not so far I couldn't walk it alone in a few hours.

I saw no one unusual thing that day. No bird flew over. I heard no movement close or far in the brush nor any animal call or cry. The landscape seemed as primed as I was for something to happen, though, its edges almost glittering they were so sharp. But night fell again and I turned in with my stomach empty and now in knots. Surely, I thought, tonight I will dream.

Awaiting sleep, kept from it by a kind of irritation, a frustrated desire for resolution, I thought my way eventually to a crossroad I knew well. On one side was this high plains country I lay in, resilient and uncapturable. In all the years I'd ridden through it, across its hills and dry watercourses, first as a boy and then as a man, it had seemed on the verge of an offering, a pronouncement. If I would but give in to it, it would speak. On the other side were what I might call the impulses of reason, the temptation to figure out every problem—personal, social, financial—the seduction behind the belief that one could engineer a solution.

I might have lain there, I knew, peeling back the layers of silence around me, until I heard the rustling and voices of animals that had lived in this place long ago, until I heard water coursing in the dry creek nearby; but I chose the opposite way. I allowed myself to feel that I had been slighted. Despite my sincerity and concentration, I had not been given anything remarkable this day to work with, no even tenuous sign to lead me on. Why not a feather, falling from a passing bird, which I would have run to catch? Or the appearance of a wolf, longer gone in this country than the grizzly? But the day had produced nothing, not even a striking stone I wanted to pocket.

Rankled, and now fully awake, I consoled myself with the thought that I had made, against the cold distance of my father and the early, violent death of my mother, a good life. I had a family coming, my work was just, and it was exactly the right work for me. I'd chosen all this deliberately, knowing the scope of my life and work would be small, but believing it would be authentic.

Where could I go from this place, then? At twenty-nine I continued to experience what I once named the Great Burden, the weird combination of oppression and challenge which grows out of knowing the incompetence of the powerful. And I believed in the possibility of work that had to be done in every corner of the world because of it. Friends in Basra and Riyadh, people I had gone to law school with, had sent me newspaper clippings about our country's empire building in Saudia Arabia and Kuwait, strategies that would one day come to a head in the oil wars. I'd grown up reading about Minamata disease, part of heavy industry's collateral damage. I'd grown up furious about

François Duvalier's Tontons Macoutes and the assassination of Juan Domingo Perón, and the killing fields of Stroessner, Pol Pot, and Suharto. The corruption of the Marcoses was a fresh memory, along with the dead of Bhopal. Against this blight I'd read biographies of Cardinal József Mindszenty and Gandhi and the South African poet Steve Biko and the Turkish writer Nazim Hikmet.

Strictly speaking, these horrors, through which people like Idi Amin and the shah of Iran moved, Cuba's Batista, Pablo Escobar's thugs, and the likes of the Contras, with their allies in banking and business, their murderous ideologies, their paranoia and hatreds, were not my affair. I was an angry bystander. I'd no power to intervene, and had no intention of dropping the work I was already committed to, not in order to raise someone else's awareness, promote greater indignation, or organize opposition. Besides, as soon as I pointed my finger at someone I knew I would flinch at the summariness of my accusation. I trusted no one with an assassination list. If I had learned one thing in the courtroom it was that corruption is never tidy. And that of all the crimes that harm society, aiding and abetting is the most insidious, the hardest to prosecute because it is so amorphous.

The world's afflictions I still consider intractable. And who, among those we might agree were the true merchants of death, who among them, really, would ever say they had been wrong and desist, go pick up the water bucket and soap, offer no defense of their acts, just go for the bulldozer, the fire extinguisher, whatever was required?

I still keep in touch with old friends from college with whom I once passionately discussed these ideas, as if our task remained realistic and definable. We have skills, we tell each other now, we've opportunity, we're reasonably well informed. We share strenuous objections to the way business and government have converged to reorganize society. Our solution so far has been to teach and apprentice, to convene opposing sides for discussion, and to circulate what government, business, and the militant religions have suppressed.

None among my friends has turned his back on the ideals of justice, which seemed so much more plausible when we were young. We've not lost faith; but for some the years have been very discouraging. Many of us can't see beyond the boundaries of our own difficulties. We're like a tribe of naked people caught suddenly in a freezing climate, men and women gathered in some sheltered hollow who have located a fire, and now spend their time in forays over a barren land scrounging for wood.

Beyond writing my briefs and arguing my cases, beyond reinforcing my friends' plans and lifting their hopes, I don't know what I am to do. What keeps me from giving up is seeing some young woman pull over to drag a dead animal off the road. Or meeting a reporter, as I just have, who has seen in the streets of Calcutta hundreds of the untended dead, curled up like leaves, who's interviewed the sleepwalking miners of Rondô- nia, the warlords of Somalia, the mujahideen, the president of the World Bank, and then sits without comment while her father complains about the price of gasoline.

What holds me is the faith of the others. What has troubled me is the exhaustion that overtakes me, the way I want no longer to be responsible.

In the morning I could again recall no dream.

Virgil was sitting in the cottonwoods when I spotted him, and birds flew from the cover of their leaves as I approached. He had half a smile. I gave him a weighted nod, as if I had something impor- tant to say, despite my too-brief stay up the creek; but we saddled our horses without saying anything.

The plains grizzly I'd seen that night on the Hi- Line, the image of it, had been heavy on my mind as I walked back down the creek. It could easily have come up off the Fort Belknap Reservation. I asked Virgil whether he thought it was likely that a rare animal like that might be safer on Indian land. Some Indians, I knew, making their own difficult transition from that culture to this, were as likely to kill the bear as any wide-eyed white boy.

"The difference between us is that what you are able to forget will not leave us alone," said Virgil. He was answering a deeper question, and I assumed he was including the bear in his "we." His tone was as close as he ever came to exasperation.

He'd seen a few plains grizzly in his life, Virgil said after a bit, one over around Boxelder Coulee and another in the Smoke Creek drainage. Both these places are on the Fort Peck Reservation.

"They're around," he said. "Everything, even the buffalo, is still around. You get to believing they're hunted out or starved out, or maybe they've run off, but as long as people are telling stories about them, as long as people keep them in their minds, they'll stay around. You have to keep telling the stories, though, calling up the memory of them. They come back in your dreams at night. They come along when you're off somewhere, walking by yourself. They're asking you why. That's their question. Why."

"My question," I tried, "would be, Why did you bring me here again?"

He didn't answer.

"I failed the first time, I failed this time."

He ignored me.

"You know what it is, Virgil? I'm a man thinking all the time. I'm a thinker. I never really stop, so most of the time whatever you're trying to teach me or show me, it can't get in."

"That's right."

"I can't be like you, Virgil."

"No, you can't. But you can answer the bear's question." He pulled his horse around to face me. "The bear is coming to you because you say you want to help, and it's you he's asking why. He's speaking for all of them out there, every animal. Why are you trying to kill me?"

"It's not me."

"You need to stop hearing your own name, Edward, whenever someone speaks."

When we got back to the truck we grained and watered the horses. After we closed up the trailer Virgil turned to me. I could see he was anxious, but his voice was so even he could have been reading a grocery list.

"That little place up there, the divide between the creeks, seems empty of spirit to you, but it isn't. You're afraid. One day I hope you go back. Maybe something will be waiting for you."

"I'm doing the best I can, Virgil."

"The bear's holding the door open, Edward. A very patient animal."

On the way back to his place, Virgil pulled over to look close where coyote tracks crossed the road.

"See here," he said, "how the front feet are digging in? He's carrying something."

I agreed.

"Looks like he crossed last night."

"Yeah." He scanned the whole of the bare blue sky, from the horizon in the east to the one in the west, before he got back in the truck.

It would be another six years before I went back up on Porcupine Creek. By then, Jill and I had two children and Virgil was in his last days in a hospital in Great Falls. I stayed in my same camp above the dry creek bed, until the voices that had so long debated the future within me grew silent, and I stepped through the door.

> Edward Larmirande, member, Métis Nation Council, attorney, author, *The Numinous Experience and the Suicide Meriwether Lewis,* on leaving Winnipeg, Manitoba

The Walls at Yogpar

I was a compulsive student as an undergraduate. After completing my studies in Han Chinese I went straight to graduate school, wanting to obtain a broad-based knowledge of—if not actual fluency in—the many other languages spoken in China, a nation oceanic in its geographical and historical reach. During those years of completely devoted study—with the Tai languages of the Southeast, the Tibeto-Burman languages of the southwest, the Turkic languages of the northwest, and the Mongol languages of the northeast—I experienced bouts of disassociation and a feeling like seasickness. I could not make sense of even an advertisement on the side of a bus. But I also knew moments of vast, almost chilling comprehension, when I could easily grasp one concept—"family," let us say—as it was imagined in eleven different languages.

Within the boundaries of the politically defined nation of "China," eighteen languages are spoken by at least 500,000 people each; another thirty-seven are spoken by lesser numbers, including Lahu (270,000), She (330,000), Uzbek (7,500), and Xibe (44,000). No one language is enough. No one can speak for all. Further, across these many borders of expression—Naxi or Salar or Dong—most cannot make themselves understood. Each of these tongues seeks to corral some bit of the fundamentally incomprehensible nature of the world—shadings of smell in the forest as they might be known to a dog, the intention behind a stranger's gesture, the origin of any single thing, the reason the heart breaks.

It is wondrous but also frightening to consider.

At the age of thirty I realized that without meaning to, I had decided against taking a permanent companion. Such a person, I thought, might too easily slow me down or misdirect my efforts. I couldn't allow myself to stop learning.

After graduate school, as I internalized more of the meaning of Chinese languages—I was fluent now in eight—I felt not only an acute appetite for unrestricted movement but a desire for unbounded physical space, an open geography. With yet another loan from my parents I moved out of my very cramped quarters in Shanghai and traveled west by train and bus, aiming for the Autonomous Region of Xinjiang, the country of Uygur and Kasak tribespeople. Given the usual mechanical breakdowns and bureaucratic interruptions, it took ten days to cross Henan, Shaanxi, and Gansu provinces. I learned to accommodate the delays, but they intensified the anxiety I felt about the fate of my books and notes, which I had shipped ahead. I often recalled the story of the *Homo erectus* fossils from Zhoukoudian Cave near Beijing, the original evidence for Peking man, all of which disappeared in a transfer between trains during World War II, never to be found.

When we finally reached the high tableland of Xinjiang, I did feel a physical relief. Here was a region larger than Alaska, bounded by great mountain ranges on three sides, with the Takla Makan, a desert as big as New Mexico, at its center. I was eager to take up my life again in this far outland, with no clear idea of what I would do. I was basically a gifted juggler of Sino-Tibetan languages. In periodic states of delirium, I believed I could actually speak the unspeakable, know the unknowable. In more practical moments I knew I was bound for employment in Urumchi, the capital city of half a million, set in the foothills of the central mountain range of the region, the Tian Shan. I could teach Han Chinese to these subjects of China and translate English technical manuals into local Uygur. In a matter of months, I believed, I could learn the other local tongue, Kasak.

In some way, I would prove useful.

. . .

Shanghai, during my years there, was much more open to the West than Urumchi was or had ever been. Urumchi had been a crossroads for Turkish, Mongol, and Tibetan traders for probably two thousand years and for other overlanders nearly as long. I was a late arrival, emblematic of the modern era, coming at a time when the city was shifting from horses and camels to assembly lines and department stores. Urumchi, though, was not as provincial as I'd initially assumed; rippling beneath the coarse bedsheets of ordinary life here, rural enough, were the strong countercurrents of its original tenants, that always fascinating and odd acumen of a truly foreign people.

I easily found work teaching at the university, also work as a translator. After settling into these routines, and an apartment, I began to tease apart the convolutions of life around me in the streets, in the newspapers, in the university, and in the manufacturing culture. I pried open life in Urumchi with confidence and ordered it, using Han, Uygur, and Manchu, a language I fell into more naturally than I did Kasak (though I would eventually become fluent in that Turkic tongue).

Being able to speak so many languages well made me, very obviously, a queer fish, even a sort of trickster figure (not to mention being Caucasian, and a woman from the West). I quickly became irritable from being stared at too long and then being called after in inappropriate ways. I missed the civility of Shanghai, where I blended in better. I tried to remind myself, of course, that I had opted for the frontier, that I just needed to develop that famous second skin, a way of knowing the world that was in keeping with speaking Manchu, Uygur, and Kasak.

My irritation at not being deferred to when it was appropriate, with not being respected, encouraged fleeting thoughts of self-doubt, which were never really far off anyway, a sense that, beyond my erudition, I had no purpose. My learning did not automatically send a signal here about the wisdom I thought I possessed. Instead it stood for self-importance, and for some probably it signaled madness. Confronted like this, I worked to keep at bay the familiar enemies of my equilibrium: loneliness, the fear that I was undesirable, the suspicion that, like a wind-up toy's, my performance would just end and people would leave.

I continued to teach language and literature, but after five months let go the translation, which had become tedious. I'd been doing most of it for local industrial concerns—oil refineries, cement plants, mining operations. Moreover, as I saw it, I was only reinforcing my employers' weirdly distorted passion for growth and material wealth. Their devotion to increased production was aggressive and humorless, menacing almost. Worker safety, pollution control, maternity leave—all this was a nuisance to them, a series of impediments to production. What was wrong with me, they asked, that I didn't work more hours? Where was my loyalty? Had I no pride?

For my employers, work had replaced the family as the locus of identity. They affected an air of tolerance with me, backward as I seemed to be, and ticked off the lists of things they had bought their families, which families were now superior to other men's.

This singular quest for expansion and personal material gain seemed a grotesque fit with general Urumchi culture outside the university and the factories. Every neighborhood was a different bolt of cloth—another color, another pattern, another weave. Tribally mixed as it was, however, and had been for centuries, life in Urumchi appeared to me everywhere a frugal (as opposed to impoverished), small-scale existence, from people's house gardens to their shops. Employment was an occasional necessity, not a defining activity.

The striving for more barrels of oil, new lodes of ore in the mountains, more deep reservoirs of water was wreaking environmental havoc in the region. It did not take me long to understand that, despite its long history as a pastoral country, northern Xinjiang Region had come to be regarded by its absentee Chinese landlords as a wasteland. As such, it was deemed best suited to mineral extraction, to gargantuan irrigation projects, and to military experiments with pathogens and poisons. It was here in dry lake depressions in the Takla Makan that the Beijing government chose to conduct nuclear weapons tests. What happened to the people of the region, to what they were attached to or aspired to be, was of no more importance to the Chinese in Beijing than it was to the local managers of the chemical plants and oil refineries.

In order to keep myself busy after I dropped the translation work, I hosted small lunches for women with traditional Turkic and Mongol backgrounds and recorded and translated their stories. They were usually older women I met on my daily walks, people I chose because they were matriarchs or had come to the city from far away, had never married, or were otherwise interesting to me. I also began compiling dictionaries, with the help of some sophisticated databases I had helped develop while I was in Shanghai. I did one of the Manchu dialect spoken by local Xibe people, an ethnic group moved in from Manchuria to act as border guards after the collapse of the Ming dynasty in 1644. Also a dictionary of Urumchi street slang, and another of the Han Chinese spoken in northern Xinjiang, a dialect heavily influenced by the Muslim backgrounds of the Uygurs and Kasaks.

It was an antic life. Some evenings, moving

slowly around the workroom in my apartment, making entries at three different workstations, I saw it as a life of ten thousand desperate distractions, no matter how calm and tidy my surfaces appeared.

Korbel Uklel lived directly below me on the second floor. It took a while to figure out what he did because he'd be gone for weeks at a time. He was a camel trader, a Kirghiz born in Kashgar. His wife and both his children had been killed in a bus accident on their way to Tashkent. One night, when we were doing laundry together in the basement, he told me he had no feelings anymore for family life. He would not marry again.

I saw Korbel casually every few weeks, but I began to look ahead to our talks. His Uygur was excellent, and for once in my life I did not treat a new friend like an informant. I didn't, in this instance, ask him to help me with his Kirghiz. So we spoke Uygur. He never pried into my life or made any even remotely inappropriate comment or effort to embrace or otherwise touch me, though I began to long for it. He took me with him once to sell camels in the market. The trappings of caravans, all the worn and antiquated equipment lying about, the smell and heat of the animals and the working demeanor of the men, stimulated me in an unfamiliar way.

I began to daydream about traveling with Korbel.

It was a ridiculous idea, I would tell myself, but I held to it tightly, and one night it took an unexpected shape. I'd chanced on a book called *Tracks* by an Australian woman named Robyn Davidson, about her crossing half that continent alone on a camel. Turning the pages and gazing at the photographs, I pictured myself in her poses, her clothing.

I wanted to cross the Takla Makan with Korbel.

The next time we met I put it to him. We were having dinner in a restaurant. (I always had the feeling when I made my bold suggestions about dinner or a movie that I was testing the limits of Korbel's Muslim faith.) He froze with the fork halfway to his mouth. Clearly it was not something he had ever considered. He was gracious about it, though. He said he would think about it, and that was the end of that part of the conversation.

My classes at Xinjiang University were full of culturally complicated young men and women, many of them from Chinese-Uygur families or Mongol-Russian families, or other mixes equally strange.

Even as I taught I could feel the traditional lines separating the languages I used in the classroom beginning to break down, as more and more workers came in with their families from Russia, Kazakhstan, Mongolia, even Kashmir. The compartmentalization of concepts I employed in organizing my dictionaries began to tremble ever so slightly in the face of these collisions and couplings. My students were streaming toward a metalanguage. I feared it might one day leave me behind.

I once read a technical paper in which the author essayed that the well-watered grasslands of northern Xinjiang, at the bases of the snow-capped Tian Shan, had been an important home to some of the earliest members of *Homo sapiens,* people who swept north tens of thousands of years ago from more temperate climes, once they had the means for making fire, clothing, shelter, and weapons. In the little traveling I'd done beyond Urumchi—west along the foot of the Borohoro Range, three hundred miles out to Bole; east from Urumchi, taking the loop road through Qitai, Qijiaojing, and Turpan, around the base of the Bogda Range—I'd found a bone-deep peace. I'd felt, strolling those grasslands, as if I'd been absolved of every error, as if the self-imposed demand to achieve had for those hours been silenced. Such relief can only come, I think, from contact with the residue, the local spirits, of ancestral humanity.

I had read some history of the Autonomous Region of Xinjiang, a countryside invaded and occupied over the course of many centuries by Arabs, Mongols, Tibetans, Huns, and recently the Chinese. After the tenth century, the region came to represent part of the great middle stretch of the Silk Road; in this way it began to play a crucial role in medieval European politics and commerce. But even as I read the fascinating particulars of these histories—the battles, the rise and eclipse of a Mongol dynasty, the midwifery of one or another technology like printing or gunpowder—it was this lone, almost stray fact—an early home for *Homo sapiens*—that stayed with me.

Even in Urumchi I felt these first people alive in the air around me, tolerant of my anxieties, my presumptions. I imagined the serenity I felt from contact with them was that serenity without which Korbel would not take me into the Takla Makan.

It was nearly a year before the subject came up again. One night on an amble, Korbel announced that we were going to cross the western end of the desert, that it had all been arranged. He was having camels sent to Aksu from Kashgar in the spring. We would parallel the road with them south to the city of Awat, on the Aksu River, then, leaving roads behind, head straight for a crossing on the Yarkand River, which would be running high with snowmelt. From there, he guessed, it might be a hundred miles or so before we picked up water again on the lower reaches of the Khotan River, flowing north out of the Kunlun Mountains. And from there, in the Tarim Basin, it would be another 150 miles to Khotan itself, a city of sixty thousand midway along the southern leg of the ancient Silk Road. Only about 300 miles, Korbel said, from Aksu to Khotan, a couple of weeks at an easy pace.

No one lived along our proposed route. "You'll be bored to death. No languages are spoken there," he joked. Once we left Awat, we would travel to the west of the Khotan riverbed, preserving our privacy by avoiding contact with any travelers who might be using this springtime shortcut across the desert, saving themselves the long turn to the west through Yarkand and Markit, where water was more dependable.

In the university library I dug out a book of landscape terms in Uygur. Over two hundred of them applied only to sand deserts, the one to the north of Urumchi and the Takla Makan to the south. That these uninhabited places of bleak stone and sand should be so highly differentiated by the Uygur took me a little by surprise. Ten or twelve terms applied to the shapes dunes assume as they migrate. Another two dozen or more applied to the inconsistent surfaces of dry riverbeds, suggesting the relative likelihood that water would be found below. Another group of terms referred to different combinations of color in bare rock outcroppings. As some of these terms for color also incorporated references to seasonal weather, I supposed they assumed an understanding that limestone, quartzite, and dolomite were each an expression of something, and that this essence changed over time, subtle as seasons were in the Takla Makan. Yet another set of terms differentiated types of loose sand, not just to distinguish areas of good footing for camels but, simultaneously, to convey something more about prevailing winds and local topography. Together, wind and ground surface sort the grains of sand by size and shape, just as they determine, working together every day, the traveler's path.

The night before we departed, Korbel showed me a map. I think he meant to reassure me about the route, as I had so many preconceived notions about the dangers. Written across it in Kirghiz in a variety of colored inks were several thousand place names. I'd never seen a map of the Takla Makan in English with more than twenty places named in the desert's interior. The map was three feet wide and seven feet long, a family heirloom. He was very proud of it.

. . .

For the first time in my life, probably, I traveled in silence. When we made camp in the afternoon I wrote in my notebook about the gait of the camels, the changing colors of the sky, and the texture and line of the desert itself. I found the Uygur geographical dictionary indispensable in sorting through complex sensations. It enabled me to write more precisely about a landscape that otherwise might have remained undifferentiated and therefore opaque in my notes. Korbel tended to the camels. He also did all the cooking and, for modesty's sake, bedded us down in separate tents, which neither of us used, preferring to sleep outside.

Korbel ignored my attempts to converse during the day, so I learned to hold my questions until we made camp. I tried to see what was around me with an eye as discerning, as discriminating, as that of the author of my dictionary. Once south of the Yarkand River it was as if Korbel and I were traveling across the ocean. As far as we could see, the raw back of the earth was a dune field of unnamed escarpments and slopes. And yet, suspecting more, I began to make out some repetitions of scale. I saw that the patterns in the dunes had a kind of rhythm to them, and so I came to appreciate the country ranging away from me smoothly in every direction as staffed notation—B-flats, C-sharps, chord changes, changes in tempo, diminuendos, rising arpeggios, and so on.

I assumed ultimately this music had all of it to do with the coming and going of the wind, its sandpapering and sweeping.

Sometimes Korbel would halt us and the baggage camels and dismount. He would point out a place where people had once made a fire. Or he would hand me up a cobble from a scatter of chert debitage uncovered by the wind, and I would see where blocks for arrow points had been knocked from the core.

I would watch Korbel as he rode, and would recall the businessman apparent in him at the market, the fastidious way he folded his clothes in the laundry room, his exasperation behind the wheel of his smoking Lada in Urumchi traffic. And now I saw him as the *dashkalem,* the caravan master, the "undisturbable and surpassing eye" leading us over the country.

A week into the trip Korbel told me I was riding well, no trouble at all for him, so we would detour a little to the east, toward an oasis called Tongguzbasti. We would soon pick up a very old route, he told me, one that ran between the Khotan, which we had by then gained, and another riverbed, the Keriya. Along the way we would see something.

That evening we crested the ridge of a dune and

I was suddenly confronted with an abandoned oasis. How Korbel had navigated the sand sea to this spot, what clues he had used, I was not able to understand even when he explained. While we sat the camels on the ridge he unfurled his map. The place was called Yogpar. All that remained was the low wall of a four-square structure with two gate-less portals, east and west. The courtyard and its well were under eight feet of sand.

Korbel said the fort dated to the time of the T'ang dynasty (deferring to my Western sense of how historical time is kept), but that it was built over walls erected during the Shang dynasty, in the second millennium before Christ. And those walls had been constructed with stones cut here before the founding of Ur, the great Sumerian city on the Euphrates. Before that, he said, he did not know, though perhaps he didn't wish to say.

Standing within the swamped walls of Yogpar, with the warm air still against my face, the stone and sand lit by a crescent moon and uncountable stars bristling in the depths of a lapis sky, I felt that same peace-to-the-bone I'd known in grasslands in the Bogda Shan. I imagined Yogpar with another name, perhaps when it, too, was a grassland, and that people traveling with dogs had thrown up skin tents here in the sea of grass against the chill of the night.

Over dinner I tried to describe for Korbel some

of the Western theory of human evolution. He nodded appreciatively but also as if my ideas might be the rivals of his own, and that his ideas, also, might be hard to grasp.

"My ancestors have been sleeping all across the Takla Makan for ten thousand years," Korbel offered. "Everywhere around us, out there and within these walls, my ancestors are sleeping. And yet, they are awake. They are the ones who keep us safe. Our agreement with them is we will provide, and they in turn will watch over us. In the morning, then, we must leave behind a little food, a little bit of our water."

I said all right, and when he did not continue I wrote in my journal for a while.

"Can you feel them, my ancestors?" he asked, sitting by in the dark.

"No," I said. "I don't think so."

"They are waiting. One day, I believe, they will speak—and then everything will change. No matter what language you speak, you will understand their meaning. You won't find water so easily after that, nor someone for your heart to fasten itself to."

I put water on the burner for tea, to let Korbel know I knew he was troubled, but also that I was grateful for this trip, for all we had seen so far. He took his tea with him when he went to check the camels. I loved the way he ran his hands over them. They were his confidants.

I was in love with him, of course, but he also represented to me a kind of man I wanted to know more about. He was as much at ease with the flow of time here as he was in Urumchi. I don't mean he was as adept at carving a new nose plug for one of the camels as he was at a computer keyboard, but that he did not seem to have a century. Depending on the context, his was a twelfth- or a twenty-first-century face. He was so little committed to the material world that I didn't doubt he could have stepped straight into the Takla Makan of a thousand years ago with no apprehension. Wherever he was he was alert to his surroundings, a habit my own culture had long since dispensed with in order to move more quickly.

He told me once that he'd been to New York, with a trade mission of some sort. He'd stayed on an extra week to have time to walk through the Fulton Fish Market and to watch the great tidal surges and currents at Spuyten Duyvil and the Battery. One evening a falcon landed on the ledge outside his hotel room window. The window was open and the bird watched him, unperturbed. He said it reminded him of some lines in a poem by Rumi, in which a perfect falcon lands on a man's shoulder in a seed market "for no reason."

He stood a moment with me when he returned. "I believe our technologies, Elizabeth, these machines we now live with, are evolving, to use your word, faster than our emotions can accommodate."

He headed for bed, but I was curious.

"Do you mean, in the face of it all, in the face of everything changing, a whole way of life gone in a generation, that we have become numb?"

"I mean that the speeding bus goes flying off the mountain road."

We bedded down in the soft, cold sand, apart from each other but within the ancient enclosure. Its low walls, barely a foot high, formed a berth, a surround against the farther dark.

I thought to tell Korbel, maybe in the morning, about a shallow cave called Teshik-Tash in the gorge of the Zautolosh River, in Uzbekistan, far to the west of our camp. Sixty-five thousand years ago, Neandertal hunters buried one of their children there, laying the body out carefully and encircling it with five or six pairs of ibex horns, which suggested to many, when the site was discovered, that the animals were its guardians. Scientists later sent the Mousterian child's bones to a museum in England. The ibex horns were put in a box and shipped somewhere else.

Who can know, now, what these people wished

the ibexes to protect the child from? Was it the scavenging of a cave hyena or something less imaginable and more dire?

Before I slept I stood atop the stone arch of the west gate and watched the wind flickering on the star-bitten edges of the dunes. But for the cold stone beneath my feet, all I could name were the constellations, my ancestors' arrangement of the stars.

Elizabeth Wangfu, translator, author, *Conquest: A Study of the International Use of American English,* member, Interasian Trade Organization, on leaving Kashgar, Xinjiang, China disassociation

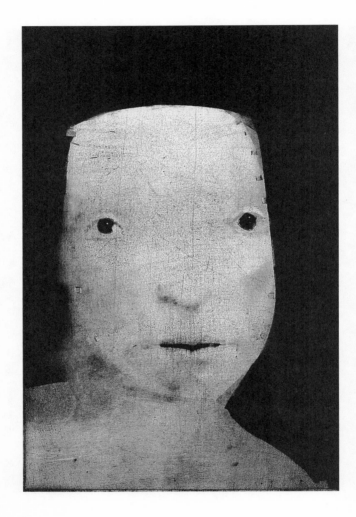

Laguna de Bay in A-Sharp

I have come to believe in my own goodwill. But do not confuse me with Mother Teresa, as I have to confess I once did. I don't have the energy she had and I don't have her gift. And really, in the time I am thinking back on, the turning point, few outside my small neighborhood knew me, had even heard of me. I didn't then, nor do I now, know the will of the Divine, or even what ordinary men and women are to do beyond courtesy toward one another, you understand, real acts of charity, and also upholding the civic virtues in our very modern world. To serve, to vote. You can choose.

In university I quickly chose African history as my major; but an opportunity arose to go to Chad during one of the famines, so I went and never came back. I couldn't comprehend the devastation. I did not understand misery until I peeked into the shabby tents to find no possessions, until one day I thought to move a body, stick limbs covered with skin and one strip of cotton, the bauble of the head. I could find no family, no friend, no one to lay claim. I did not know where to carry it. I stayed in that camp for a year. I could have stayed for ten.

God, I suppose, wanted those bodies.

It was not the evidence of slow starvation in that first camp that took such fierce hold of me, that so outraged me, but the indifference I encountered all around it. I grew up thinking hate the opposite of love, but it is indifference that is the opposite of love. In Chad, no one had even a piece of paper to write down the names of the dead. Not a twig to heat water. Not a match to light the twig. Oh yes, you could say that some man or woman, this group or that in government, was to blame; and, of course, relief food was sometimes delivered to the wrong homes in N'Djamena, where, let us say, it fed the household pets of the wealthy; and yes, of course, what the television journalists from Europe and North America spent on their desert wardrobes, on sunscreen and cosmetics and their hair, would have bought us enough millet to feed a camp of one thousand for a week, would have paid for fifty truckloads of water. And certainly visitors took more food than they left. But this is ordinary selfishness. It is simple-mindedness, the industry of charity at work. This is not evil.

This oblivion was not the problem.

It was the shape of the indifference, the failure

to love. This absence will take anyone down after a while, in any corner of the world. So, the television cameraman who, out of his own pocket, shipped us two crates of food from Andalusia when he got home; or the bureaucrat who came down from N'Djamena with no entourage, no announcement, only a truckful of briquettes he had picked up somewhere, who brought his own pots and pans and cooked for a day in the equatorial sun—these men engaged the impossible paradoxes of the famine camps, understood the choices the street beggars have. Their love was imperfect, but they were willing to acknowledge their complicity. I remember thinking at the time that they were with us.

As I saw it then, indifference began by accommodating the impulse to affix blame. It grew out of the need to separate oneself from the brutality one witnessed. It was the need, for expediency's sake, to make the suffering an abstraction. I still see it this way. It was one of the things that did not change over the years.

My mother was born in May Pen, Jamaica, but grew up with her physician parents in Back Bay Boston. She met my Brahmin father at Harvard, on his way to becoming an influential and high-powered attorney, a position she would achieve a few years after him. Looking back, I have to admire the way they defeated or just passed around the scrutiny and curiosity they attracted as a well-to-do mixed-race couple. My two brothers and I, on the other hand, felt challenged by our situation. We became confrontational—bullies. We had down pat all the sixties rhetoric of indictment. The three of us argued often about who the culprits actually were. Complacent middle-class blacks? Racist white aristocrats? I'm embarrassed to recall it.

When I was twenty and in the famine camps, I was certain I was coming close to identifying an enemy. I wrote many letters of accusation and indignation to governments and institutions like the International Monetary Fund. But in this haranguing frame of mind I only added to the burden of those around me. I saw my way as the way of the lover, and I was certain it was the only and true way. I thought I was an emissary of God. I was the emissary of myself, of course.

A year in Chad and I grew so disaffected I became almost violent. My position was righteousness. Anger was my food. (Many young samaritans go through this. Your valor and ethics in these days are less endearing to people than you believe.) I returned to North America behaving as if no one else had ever been to Africa. Like an underappreciated man facing a typhoon alone, I labored to establish a Médecins Sans Frontières of my own. I expounded and moralized with institutions to get them to help me reduce suffering in the world. My plans were as grandiose as my ambition. Believing I was a visionary, I disdained the time-consuming work of describing, for these potential donors, exactly what I would do. I left the details to people enthralled with my imagination.

I always kept human suffering in the realm of abstraction back then, thinking if I didn't I wouldn't be able to function. I affected a roguish demeanor and, hoping to recruit them to my cause, I sought out old friends at school. I accepted any request to speak.

In those early years I could not understand why women did not fall deeply in love with me, why they were not taken with my compassion for the world, attracted to my knowledge of foreign cultures, my sophisticated politics. It was, of course, because there was no room for them, though quite some time would pass before this became clear to me.

Then I met Minty. At the time I was working for the International Red Cross, mostly as a disaster-relief camp manager, traveling in that particular year from Venezuela to Cameroon to Pakistan and Irian Jaya, having failed in a two-year effort just before that to revamp field operations for the World Health Organization. Minty was a Christianized Dinka from Sudan, very tall, very black, very musical. In my view, initially, he did not sufficiently appreciate the intellectual and social strengths, the savviness I believed I brought to the work he and I did. But it was that he was just tolerating me.

Minty had lived with war nearly all his life. His body bore the ritual scarring of his initiation and the scars of a bystander to violence. He had lost three fingers in a bus bombing and an ear when he walked into a firefight in an alley in Juba. I thought he was not a serious enough man to be considered a professional in our work. Too often with him it was battery-powered music or impromptu dance. It never seemed the right thing. But in those days I thought gravity was the key to all our success.

I met Minty in Addis Ababa, where he was an assistant to the camp manager, and then worked with him later in Sri Lanka; but I did not get to know him until we traveled to Paris together. He took me to Cirque du Soleil and to some jazz clubs in Montmartre. He got to know a different kind of people in a strange place than I did, people more at ease in their skins, people like the musicians and the trapeze artists who were after some erotic moment in which sensitivity and action fit perfectly together. Minty, striking up conversations and traveling with half the luggage I thought essential, opened up my life on that trip. Compared to him, I had been very crudely in pursuit of what life offered.

It was with Minty that I quit trying to know and began trying to be, is one way to put it. It was with Minty that I came to understand that you cannot eliminate evil through reorganization. "You think like a commando," he told me once. "With you it is always strategic this and tactical that. We are not at war, my friend." And then he'd laugh.

Laughter—that was something I had entirely missed, to find hilarity inside the grotesque. It did not come overnight, the transformation this insight precipitated. Indeed, in the beginning I thought something had been taken away from me. And then I worried that my urge to laugh was actually a sign of indifference or madness. If the suffering is so funny, I would wonder, why do we bother with compassion? You can see, possibly, that I was almost getting it. When I lay awake at night I would try to remember, for example, whether Job had ever laughed.

That was a long time ago, years when I felt the world was tipping over and that only I and a few others were keeping it from breaking completely apart. Minty died of hepatitis B in the same month my oldest brother was killed fighting alongside Cuban soldiers in Angola. I am not ashamed to say I missed Minty more. He made his life up out of almost nothing. No appetite, no idea seemed to possess him. My brother was a reminder of a family where each sibling was the aggressive missionary of his own truth, and no one of us wanted to be the other's convert.

Minty had nothing to sell.

These were the long middle years of reassessment for me. I quit the Red Cross and, for reasons I cannot entirely understand even now, entered Union Theological Seminary in New York. I had been raised Roman Catholic but had drifted far from that practice. For me, Christianity operated like an irascible and reactionary parent. It didn't want to make the acquaintance of anyone outside its own neighborhood; it didn't want to face overpopulation if that would mean contraception or abortion; and it threw its hands up over the liberation theology of Gustavo Gutiérrez and the process theology of John Cobb and Thomas Berry. Talk of the rewards of the earth set it to drumming its fingers on the table, impatient as it was for the rewards of heaven.

Christianity as a philosophy, however, also vigorously championed the ideals I had so ferociously embraced as a youth—compassion, forgiveness, spiritual ecstasy. At the seminary I kept my distance from the rituals of Christianity, but I read closely the work of spiritual scholars like Elaine

Pagels and Leonardo Boff and novelists like Shūsaku Endō and Graham Greene. I was trying to penetrate to the roots of what I might claim as my own: the meaning of sacrifice, the passion of the historical Jesus.

I took with me the question of a passionate altruism and a nonreligious devotion to the Divine, but put the seminary, with what I felt were its detachments from the world, behind me.

I went to San Francisco, where a friend from college living in the East Bay needed a house sitter. I spent my nights in a few clubs in Oakland where the music was very good, some jazz trios right up there with the ones Minty and I heard on our first trip to Paris, and during the day I gravitated toward the Oakland docks. I was feeding the romance of shipping out, and when my friend returned, I did. I sailed with containerized cargo for Inchon, three hours before sunrise on a cold, wet night, with no plan but to keep going.

Ships' crews are rough and cynical. It's another sort of destitution than I'd known, the men victims neither of famine nor war but caught in travail nevertheless. Employed for globalization, meant to escort and guard an accumulation of goods they are not permitted to touch. They have all the attributes of the marginalized: despair masked by detachment, self-hatred masked by humor, capitulation masked by shows of defiance. In the ports theirs is a search for bliss and unconsciousness, an escape from memory.

I tried to meet eye to eye and shake hands with all my crewmates, especially those who did not trust me, which were most. I worked hard, I listened, I didn't take unreasonable offense, and insofar as I understood, gave none. The old virtues. When we were in port I bought local recordings of local music for our shipboard music library. I bought local food and cooked aboard the ship for whoever wanted a change. I got some of my watch away from the port and out into the countryside to see people working with not very much—a worldwide way of makeshift life as amazing to the eye as a desert river in high flood. Also, for the first time in perhaps five or six years, I began to visit hospices again, to see if I could recomprehend charity, about which I had once been so ruthless. The ships I came to feel comfortable in mostly worked the East China and South China seas—Singapore, Hong Kong, Manila, Haiphong, Shanghai. In those cities I got to know some of the hospice workers and through them witnessed, once again, the physical damage caused by the humiliations of industrial manufacturing, the Western plan to create wealth.

I wished in my reveries to be like Minty, free of any need to judge, acting as a vessel of forgiveness and joy; but it was these very things that formed a final barrier for me. I withheld my joy if I wasn't sure of my company. I judged and brooded. And I prayed to Minty as though he were a saint.

There was no single event in the rhythm of doing physical work, riding out the storms, and gazing to sea, no apocalyptic moment of change, but one day I realized I no longer had any desire to be recognized. This one thing, not having to be singled out for adulation, was the beginning of a new awareness. I might put it this way: I was no longer afraid of immersion in the unvarnished world. I no longer needed to be regarded as a man with campaign ribbons from the most just of human wars. Or even to be recognized as a smart fellow. All I needed to do now was to reduce somewhat the level of suffering where I encountered it, to moderate the levels of cruelty to which so many remained inured. I still wanted such people—the indifferent—to be held accountable. I wanted someone to entreat with them and subject them to the spirit of the law. But mine was no longer the voice to do it. I had no more plans for reorganization and reconstruction. I had nothing, anymore, to sell.

On a trip to Calcutta in 1991 I met Mother Teresa. Like Minty she broke down further my sense of what was right, of what had to happen, by entering the misery around her instead of trying to beat it into submission. I don't know about sainthood, but I would have to say she was owned by no one but God, and that her God was as ecumenical as the air we inhaled. She took me with her into the streets— or I followed her; she was not an instructor in that sense—and I saw unfold there what must have occurred in Galilee all those centuries ago. Her incomprehensible compassion and ministration, anonymous as water.

I got off the ships for good in Manila, during the last year of Corazon Aquino's presidency. I had no goal after that but to encounter the destitute, to offer a few words of condolence, eye to eye, hand to hand, and for that moment to have no separation between us because of race or other circumstance. Sometimes, with the elderly, I would try to wash a face. I provided as I could. Through a retired ship captain I got a job as an orderly in the Cancer Detection Center at Quezon Memorial Hospital. The income from that job helped with everything.

There was something else I had thought about, too, ever since Minty and I went to Paris. It was the way that music broke you up and held you, how it tripped up fear's great authority over life, how it put you back in the world you were sometimes so desperate to leave. From those days on I traveled with tapes of Hubert Laws, Chick Corea, Jaco Pastorius, and the others. I listened in my room on West Eighty-ninth Street when I was in the seminary and on the ships and on night shift at the hospital. And then I took what was for me a bold step. I had some limitations to contend with at my age, but I learned to play the tenor sax. Sonny Rollins. Roland Kirk. Charles Lloyd. I thought if I could get three or four compositions down from their repertoires, and learn to improvise, if I could play out in a field at night so the tones would just carry to distant rooms with their windows open, it would be like that night in Montmartre had been for me, when a friend cracked open the shell in which I had been content to see but never actually meet the world.

> Jefferson deShay, physician, social historian, editor, *The Correspondence of Corazon Aquino,* three volumes, on leaving Cagayan de Oro, Mindanao, the Philippines

Níłch'i

Like many young men on the run from the threat of leading a common existence, I spent the early years of my adult life in very remote regions of the earth—the Tanami Desert, the Chukchi Sea, the Kalahari scrub. I tried to move on foot through those geographies with a level of awareness so sharp I would leave no trace of my passing. I strove to be invisible. The tolerance of those I traveled with—it was their country, always—was great, and of course I was a source of amusement to them. I was naive, but so were they; and I was trying to solve a problem they had not yet heard of.

My schooling was exceptional, if you think of it in terms of the quality of the teaching and my exposure to the wellsprings of Western ideas— Hotchkiss, Yale, graduate work in anthropology at Stanford. However, I wasn't able to extract from this instruction what I needed to live. I could *make* a good living, but something essential always appeared to me to be missing. Think of a mountain lake somewhere, caught in a flattering light—a stunning scene, but then you learn the lake holds no fish. Think of a marriage with no moments of abandon. If I'd gone into religious studies instead of anthropology, perhaps life would have unfolded very differently for me; but unless I had actively broken with my traditions, I would have been trained to follow the theologies of redemption—Judaism, Christianity, Islam. The presumption there is that though humanity has started off badly and is burdened with sin, it can achieve a state of perfection through diligence and self-improvement.

I was more taken with theologies of creation. The world is beautiful and we are a part of it. That's all. Our work is not to improve, it is to participate. I was a long while coming to an understanding of these thoughts, and in my late teens and early twenties I thrashed about in the confines of my own ignorance and fears.

I was too young, during those times of disaffection, to have taken up one of the Eastern religions, for example, as anything more than trappings, a costume. Overall, I would have to say I simply didn't trust organized religion, most especially what American and English missionaries pushed so aggressively on the people of other countries. When I watched my mother prepare for church on

Sunday mornings, I would detect someone shaping the many disappointments of her life into a stance, an attitude toward God that was dutiful, if reproving. God, on occasion, was a disappointment to her. Our High Episcopalian position was not an expression of faith, it was a hedge against theological eventualities. We approached the realm of religion as a patrician accountant might suffer the questions of some agent of the authorities. Our approach lacked joy, certainly, also sincerity. And forget about the ecstasy of St. Teresa, the mysticism of St. John of the Cross.

My father emphasized from the start that I could be a success in life with a quite simple formula. My schooling, along with an introduction to men in business and government, together with a suitable financial initiation into adult life, would all be provided; my only responsibilities, my father would say pointedly, were to do well in school and to conduct myself in public in such a way as to be worthy of the endowment. No scandal, no excesses.

My father was, and is, no fool. I have to say he is a loving man, a husband and father devoted to his family's welfare, though the issue of the family's welfare was generally murky and always, for me, ominous. Initially, my father and I were very close; now it's as if we had been born into separate families, separate cultures. It's most often a risk to assume what someone else might believe, but I think my father remains hugely puzzled about why I declined to accept all that he once offered. When I was eighteen I couldn't explain my resistance to him. I didn't have clear reasons, and I had no life experience to call on, to make my half reasons resonate. In my twenties the argument from reason lost its appeal. And by then I'd ceased to feel any need to explain the path I'd taken.

I was probably insufferable in my self-righteousness, arguing with my parents, a bore in my angry young man's stance. But I was only earnest in trying to show them—and myself—that I was to be taken seriously. Nothing in the way we lived prepared me for what I felt compelled to do. And because trying to say what that was only made me sound like a fool, it increased the distance between us.

On their side, my parents gave up trying to make a place for me in their world, a decision that hurt more than I allowed them to see. I wished they'd asked what place I wanted to have, instead of reacting with so much exasperation and a sense of being imposed on when I didn't accept what they thought would work for them. They seemed to think the issues that lay at the heart of their life— fidelity to law and custom, formal education, social standing, vigorous patriotism—were goals I was indifferent to or despised. That wasn't so. With some allowance for interpretation, I shared their ideals.

My mother made all this especially hard. She dismissed as ludicrous any friend of mine whose politics or religion (let alone diction or way of dress) was not in keeping with her own. With my houseguests she was barely civil if they were not obviously wellborn, Protestant, and white. Her scorn for what I valued cut so deep it created doubts I couldn't throw off. I was well into my thirties, and long gone from home, before I could see her condescension as anything other than cavalier disdain. It was, instead, her nearly frantic fear of what was unfamiliar. It was so strong it made her want to set fire to the thing.

Our falling out, predictably, came over the war in Vietnam. My father told me that if I didn't want to go, I needn't. He could arrange that. But to run to Canada or to register as a conscientious objector would be disastrous. His premise was that once I got the "rebellion" out of my system, I meant to have a life like his; and he worried that wouldn't be possible after such a flagrant and unsophisticated denunciation of the country's official position.

I always had the feeling in our please-come-into-my-study discussions—after I'd helped organize protests in the San Joaquin Valley with the United Farm Workers; the time right before I left for graduate work in anthropology, when he said I was beginning to take too serious an interest in Indians; and when I quit the lacrosse team in my senior year at Yale after I was elected captain—I always felt he was reviewing my life like a faithful family attorney who'd resigned himself to preparing a cantankerous witness. The testimony he wanted to nudge out of me might have fallen well on the ears of men like those who sat on his board of directors, but it wasn't my language.

It was hard for me to acknowledge to him back then that his carefully reasoned objections to my plans often made me think them through again, and sometimes to change my mind. With regard to the war in Southeast Asia, the reconsideration he forced resulted in a profound change. As much as I wanted to be viewed by others as a CO, as convincing as I could be defending that position, the truth was I was not. Somewhere deep in my tissues I believed in all the simplistic abstractions upon which the country had been founded, in the high Enlightenment principles of justice and equality. And I further accepted that these principles were threatened by Vo Nguyen Giap's Vietcong and Ho Chi Minh's design to reunite the Vietnams under Communism.

On a cold February morning in New Haven, a few months before I graduated, I boarded a bus for New York and at the Thirty-fourth Street Armory went through a daylong military physical. At the time, 1966, assuming you would be drafted anyway, opting for an early physical would allow you to pick the branch of the military you wanted to serve in. I'd chosen to train as an army medic. I would not kill anyone except in self-defense. Instead, I would try to evacuate and save the wounded. To my astonishment and relief I did not pass the physical. Torn cartilage in my knees, they said. Lacrosse.

The graduate work in anthropology I was then completely free to pursue led me to believe that while human cultures are markedly different—and that you ignored those differences at your peril—some human social arrangements were so widespread and so enduring that to dismantle them seemed at least risky, if not stupid. The central problem in my imagination, given that people were social animals, was this: How much latitude could a society give an individual without threatening its own fabric? When my father told me to make something of myself, he meant, not incidentally, for me to mold around myself a family that would direct its energies toward what *I* hoped to accomplish. It would be *my* decisions that would set the tone and direction of the lives of my wife and children. Of course, this arrangement broke down repeatedly in my father's time, precipitating divorce and other kinds of ruinous harm and violence. But he was not changed in his belief.

I asked him once what it meant to "provide" as a spouse. "Food on the table, money in the bank," was his instant answer. This was his gospel, but I don't think it was what he actually believed. What my father adhered to and what he believed were not always the same thing, and in that difference was the source of his fury when life didn't go according to his plan. If I had suggested to him that to provide for his family might mean the type of commitment that translated into time spent at home—if I'd even been able to frame that thought—it would have forced his towering indignation, my suggestion being read as an accusation.

We reached out to each other a hundred unsuccessful times.

What I could never make clear to my father was that I did not believe he owed me any explanation for the shape of his life. In my view, the basic arrangements of social organization for human beings—drawn from ten thousand years or more of family and village life—had been changed so radically and so swiftly over the last hundred years by the demands of industrialization that the benefits of these long-established arrangements were now forgotten.

We are together on a careering ship, I wanted to suggest to him. We need to be loving and frank, even if we cannot agree about the necessary repairs.

We have to be fearless about facing what I had once told him was an unbankable future.

He hated the idea—which I constantly forced on him—that by comparison with traditional, indigenous communities Americans were a lonely and unhappy people. For him, the quality of anyone's possessions was a fair indication of the quality of that person's life. If your belongings were meagre, your shelter spare, your art scant, your food unrefined, your history uneventful, your system of transport not mechanized, your philosophy undebated, if all you'd done was endure, he saw nothing to admire.

He told me it was envy that drove the editors of foreign newspapers to routinely disparage American culture, to write that it hinged on constant distraction, on the promotion of anxieties, disorders, and thwarted dreams that consumerism could easily fix.

"Which of these editors," he said to me one night, "would ever refuse my circumstances if they were offered."

He spoke like an addict, God forgive me.

It was long ago that we had these disagreements. The last one, the breaking apart, was about patriotism. "A patriot stands with his country, especially in troubled times, even when he doubts the wisdom of the path chosen by those in power," he would reiterate for me. "He doesn't call for the reinvention of society, he doesn't promote divisive statements or make incendiary remarks."

I argued for another sort of patriotism, one that did wonder aloud whether allowing business so strong and so legally unrestrained a voice in government would take our experiment in democracy into the sea.

My father and I could find no way to love each other, except by seeking refuge in the memory of our early life together, where there was no conflict. We assumed, without wishing to think more on it, that following on those years something had simply gone wrong.

My children now find in me, I am certain, the flaws I once saw in him. Intransigence. Denial. I am mortified, not just embarrassed, to have to admit that in some fundamental way I have failed, both as a father and as a spouse. My determination to succeed came to an unforeseen end, which defeat there is no escaping.

For a long while the five of us were a rebellious crew. We shared a radical politics and expressed ourselves in public forums in similar ways: respectfully confrontational, morally adamant, politically skeptical. But I—or we—could not love each other as we had hoped. We unraveled. And then the children's mother and I decided to end it. She and I shared a kind of bewilderment in addition to the sadness, bitterness, and relief that were to be expected. We could not explain it to the children. We had planned to make a difference. Beyond petty flare-ups of frustration that came in a particular moment during the formal dismantling of our family, it could be said that no one was asked to shoulder the major blame, and no one sought revenge. We took pride in that.

We wanted, but in the eyes of our friends did not get, an exemplary divorce. Our lawyers, like soldiers, preferred combat to negotiation. They went after, exacerbated, and then exploited the otherwise unremarkable unhappiness everyone feels over the circumstances of life.

I didn't think I would ever marry again after that. The emotional devastation was complex and enormous. Like any wounded animal I sought refuge and, predictably, I had several short-lived romances while I moved steadily toward a deeper need. That need was to seek out a particular set of circumstances I had been considering for many years and then think them through carefully.

In my twenties I'd read a book about the concept of wind—the movement of air—in Navajo philosophy. I'd made some notes and then put the book aside with the idea of returning to it one day. I treated it as a marker in the sort of future I was trying to imagine for myself.

According to Navajo belief, winds exist all around and also within a person. Together these winds constitute an invisible entity, and the entity is understood as something holy. Other native North American peoples have refined similar ideas; but the Navajo conception is particularly successful in relating the idea of the individual to the concept of a stable society. "The wind standing within one," as the Navajo express it in English, is in constant motion, in two ways: in respiration, the breathing in and out of air, and also by continuously passing through skin whorls on the fingers and toes. A Navajo adult moving gracefully through the world—someone who signifies harmony through his behavior and emotions, and so, in the Navajo mind, beauty—is seen as someone steadied by wind moving between the toes and the ground, between the fingertips and the sky.

The Navajo believe that through *nítch'i* (Holy Wind), individuals participate in graces or powers that surpass those of the individual, and that those graces or powers keep one secure in the world and confirm one's indispensability, one's necessity in the world. The most dreadful thing imaginable would be for *nítch'i* to withdraw its support from a human being. *Nítch'i* is seen as the primary source of the breath, thought, speech, and light that, together, create beneficence around us.

Like every people, the Navajo are trying with this metaphor to provide a name and imagery for some force invisible but essential to life. And for them, not incidentally, this metaphor is not a metaphor, as we have it. It is the truth.

For many years, as the Navajo might say if they cared to, the wind was a pathetic breeze in me, or even a stillness sometimes, I suppose. Occasionally during that time I actually imagined my confusions and disaffections as the state of being "out of breath." If I could only get my breath back, I would think, I might be able to view the misfortune of my divorce and the estrangement from my father as microcosms of what I was trying to understand, on a much larger scale, about the wayward nature of my culture. (So much of it for me came down, one way or another, to the failure to love.)

Nítch'i hwii' siz̨íinii, "the Wind within one," is not conceivable as discrete in the sense of being an individual soul. This makes our vexing question of how one fits into the world meaningless. A person can't not fit. Nor is one able to achieve the distance from life necessary to experience existential loneliness. Instead, all one's efforts are bent toward enhancing and balancing the experience of feeling included in life.

The notion of my now going somewhere to consult with Navajo singers about these matters seems more than just naive. It would be impertinent. In any case, traditional Navajo would be apt to deny they could help. It's the wind, they'd say, that's the teacher. I can't be satisfied at this juncture of my life, however, with just passively accepting the idea that the wind is a kind of world soul. I need the wind itself, the actual being outside my control, as a teacher, in the same way I required as a young man the real ground from which to learn, the empirical event over the imaginary thought.

Therefore, with the knowledge and blessing of my former wife and the children, whom I still honor, still need, I will now go away for a while. As with my similar, earlier immersions in books—histories, academic and popular studies, novels— which always preceded the working out of any formal, considered statement I wanted to make, I will now search out the longest-known and most dependable of the earth's winds. The harmattan of Algeria, I will find that. The sirocco of Calabria, I will encounter it. The trades of Martinique, the katabatics of Antarctica, the simoon of Iran, the onshores of the Atacama and the Namib. I will stay with them.

I've no illusions about being Navajo or even understanding fully what they know. I am Caucasian. I was raised to be a member of the upper class of New England and am comfortable accepting that history. It is specifically to that group of people, moreover, the hardest for me to accept, that I wish to return. I have to find a language they can accept, an experience they will trust. But I believe this too will be there when I put my face into these winds. I believe there is more here than the Navajo idea with which I begin.

I hope I do not make a fool of myself.

Marion Taylor, alternative energy consultant, producer, *Changing Woman's Sons,* on leaving Dar es Salaam, Tanzania

Flight from Berlin

The morning of the spring equinox I watched first light wash over the jungled hills above the Utala River. I leaned into the brace of my hands splayed against the red granite wall, absorbing the needle mist of warm water between my shoulder blades and peering sideways at the flush of golden light. With the light's bloom, the chill air began to dissipate and the steam of life to rise: slow fog skimming the clear Utala, cloud banners drifting in the green canopy of the jungle forest, my breath billowing, condensation misting the shower glass.

I am going to move on soon, maybe as soon as tomorrow. I've sensed disappearing may be necessary now—I've been on the Web quite a bit, following news of my country in the national and foreign press. But I'll be moving on because it's the right thing for me. I've been restored here. I'm finished.

I've brought my coffee to the veranda and set it

steaming on the solawood table, together with sharpened pencils and a few sheets of pulpuna paper. At this early hour, in this latitude at this season, sunlight pries from shadows on the riverbank below a life that cannot at other times be seen. I've been recording facets of it, as far as my skills go. Together with my notes on these animals and descriptions of the physical setting, I've been forwarding the drawings to scientific journals, where their occasional publication—I'm speaking here of the most marginal of journals—has stirred some objection and criticism. Not an accomplished-enough naturalist, they say. Not a skilled-enough illustrator.

Already the equatorial light has cast the wood grain of my drawing board into a pattern of razor-edged shadows, isolating them between planes of light grading from matte to glare. Can I get this same depth into my drawing, this same suggestion of life?

It's not sunlight drowning darkness in my room that awakens me but the sonic shift from night to day. The distant, headlong tones of the plunging river at this time of year are pierced, first, by the ripple calls of paladin birds and the shriek and bark of magimbas, small primates that live on fruit alone, in the uppermost branches of the jungle forest's trees, and that never descend to the jungle floor. Then come the extended trills—twenty seconds sometimes—of clarindas, and the grating cough notes of gotts. Flocks of dits prattle-chirping. The morning quickly effervesces into a rarified chorus no one can easily separate. It's all one water.

I'm sitting several hundred feet above the Utala, on an outcrop of metamorphic rock black after a night rain but with broad veins of gleaming lapis lazuli running through it, on a platform of cedar planks which some Tukano boys put together for me, shortly after I came here. I shut my eyes now for minutes at a time, to concentrate more deeply on the perfume of orchids and ridisses braided through the current of night air still falling down the valley. As soon as I understood from the Tukano that the fragrances released by particular flowers alleviated certain kinds of pain, I began growing these flowers near the house. I'd always assumed we smelled flowers for pleasure, but the Tukano say that the habit of putting the face to a flower is actually founded in a need for palliatives. The pleasure comes from the overall sensation of interacting with the plant.

I experience pleasure in the first inhalation from an unfamiliar orchid, they tell me, because I am retrieving the memory of a conversation from long ago, one that left me feeling exhilarated. Similarly, if a first inhalation makes me snort and turn away, that is from a conversation that went bad.

I play a sort of game with the sweet-smelling

ridisses. Early in the morning I try to pry out of the stream of air at least half a dozen species of this lily, inhaling slowly from the standing wave of turbulent air running over the rock outcrop on which the house sits. I'll recognize *Ridis paloma*, forest dove ridiss. *Ridis uxoris. Ridis conlacrimis. Ridis stygis.* One morning I teased out twelve. A friend, a woman named Aweseela, can get more, but she says with a tolerant laugh like your grandmother's that I am coming along.

I dissect the riverbank with binoculars now, alert for the movement of yatira and ohimba, and watching for spenamores, which I know will emerge in the coming hour. (My sketches, my notes on the wafting landscape of the jungle's smell, my reports on animal behavior, my phonic renditions of birdcalls—all this goes into the house's *liberdomus* for the next occupant.)

Most of my life, I've been one to say, "I wouldn't have believed it unless I'd seen it." Not long after I had come to Dowilda the thought reversed itself. It became, "If I hadn't believed it, I wouldn't have seen it." This was the step: I trusted Aweseela and the other Tukano people. They didn't attempt to turn me against my own culture, and they nursed me through a deadly bout of fever. They taught me how to live "quietly" in their part of the Curiouriari River country. In time I came to doubt nothing they said, even if my reasoning gave them nowhere to stand.

I quickly lay in head profiles of a couple of yatiras. I've had to develop an unfamiliar confidence in order to work this fast, no hesitation in my line, no pondering between strokes. Once, I might have described this as drawing by instinct, but it's quite different. The "object" to be drawn is not an object, in the sense that an artist is able to impose his scrutiny on it. The only way this will work—the quick study that seems so exactly right, a rendering inexplicably beyond the artist's technical skill—is if the artist is in conversation with the "object." Drawing by dialogue, you might call it. The artist engages the subject of the drawing as his equal and, through some shared faculty, it contributes.

My understanding—say in this instance this morning—is that one of the yatiras is responding to my interest and the drawing is a visible record of our exchange. Also, as it becomes apparent that a drawing will be no better than the quality of the conversation, you learn to bear down. Early on, my mind would wander. I'd feel a twinge of embarrassment, see the drawing as a failure, and try to start over. Most often I could, but occasionally the opportunity would simply vanish. However, once I gained an awareness of what the Tukano call "quiet" life, an ability to discern the half-visible life of the forest, once I became capable of working on that level, I never again lost the power to relocate the conversation—with a stone, the river, a tree, one of the "quiet" animals, or one of the creatures—a macaw or ocelot—most everyone would notice. I could always defeat the distraction.

I got down three very nice sketches of the yatiras' profiles while the pair ambulated over tree roots and an ohimba dittered away close by with a groundnut. More, of course, always waits to be done. Years of such mornings and I'll have gotten down a lot of conversation, say the Tukano, but nothing definitive.

Aweseela tells me, from what I've explained to her, that my people have mostly "written down" only the "loud" conversation with things in the world. When I asked her once to be more specific, she took my drawing paper and with only eight or ten strokes rendered the character of my house. She revealed it as conspicuous and forward, a bullying presence, despite the efforts I'd made to get it to blend in with the line and color of the rock and jungle around it.

When I finally put the pulpuna sheets aside, I recalled something from the time I felt, like many others, that my life served no purpose. Do you remember any such days? It was as though we all lived in tunnels then, crowded in with some stranger's furniture, with more furniture arriving all the time. For me, the terrifying part was the ease with which you could lose your imagination—just abandon it, like a gadget. Everything was supplied, even if you had to pay for it all. We were told things would run more smoothly—less crime, less disease, less unhappiness, less trouble—if everyone stuck to the same plan, pursued identical goals. What made me want to run was the ease with which people gave in.

In every quarter of life, it seemed then, we were retreating into fundamentalism. The yes/no of belief, the in/out of fashion, the down/up of pharmaceuticals, the on/off of music, the hot/cold of commitment, the dead/live of electricity, the forward/backward of machinery, the give/take of a deal. Anyone not polarized became an inconvenience for management and its legions of loyal employees. People endorsed the identification of enemies and their eradication, just to be rid of some of the inevitable blurring.

We didn't hear enough then about making the enemy irrelevant. No one said, loud enough to be heard over the din of pacification, Let's make something beautiful, so the enemy will have one less place to stand.

The year before I came to South America I went to Berlin with my family. I met with seventeen like-minded friends and acquaintances. With a half-dozen translators, without whom we would never have gotten our information sorted, our complex emotions conveyed, our promises made, we persevered. We couldn't get anywhere deep, however. We were like agitated bees, all hovering around the same flower, looking for a way in.

I had no answers in Berlin. I couldn't identify that flower. I was tired of trying. I didn't want to save anyone or anything anymore. Lebensraum was what I wanted, please forgive me, freedom from the suffocating interlock of venal desire, dire warning, Teutonic competition, extreme overreach, and sophisticated oblivion that had become, in the dim tunnels back home, everyday life.

I remember I had a book with me in my hotel room, *The Season of the Catapult.* The author had created an impoverished futuristic world in which the violent action of a Roman military machine, the catapult, symbolized political forces at work in the culture. To operate the catapult, men winched down a pivoted arm with a windlass mounted on a wheeled carriage, locking it under spring tension. With the device now cocked, they loaded a basket at the far end of the arm with an array of debris—tree stumps, boulders, dead animals, shrapnel iron, broken pipe, bottles of oil stoppered with lit fuses. When the arm was cut loose, the debris was hurled with terrific force toward the target—a street jammed with people, the walls of a shrine, a loaded granary, livestock pens.

In the author's fictional world, those who owned and managed the catapults conquered and ruled; those who loaded and operated the catapults, who pulled them hither and yon in harness, earned a provisional safety; all the rest of society lived at risk. The catapult was an instrument of terror. For some who followed its wanderings, the catapult's regular deployment against people, the carnage it created, was a form of entertainment. From the rubbish it scattered, those fleeing its destruction often rigged part of their living.

Sitting there in the hotel room in Berlin, the book finished, I wished the invincible catapult masters of the book had agreed to leave some quarter of the world untouched, so, projecting myself into the book, I might go there with my family and never again have to think about scenarios of enforcement. I wished I could see a way—I was pushing far beyond the author's intentions here, I suppose, but for me her allegory spoke directly to the drama of that time—see a way to suggest to the catapult masters of my own time that it was the catapult, not its owners, that was now writing our history. The masters were pursuing lebensraum not for themselves but for the machines. The machines were living for the attention they got. They lived to disrupt. They fed on corruption. You could see that they hated anything beyond their control, like beauty.

But, the masters would counter, it is too simple a device to take so seriously. They would argue they could unrig the catapult whenever they wished, render it useless. But then, I might have asked, what would the masters do with their lives? Without the machine, what would be their calling?

I could have been a catapult master, in a trice. When you are worn out, dictatorial powers—it makes no difference whether you are the victim or the perpetrator—exert an attraction. Giving in is so much more appealing than going on. Like the catapult masters, I had confused possessing something with being in control of it; and I had underestimated the power of what I had created. I was part of the juggernaut against which I was fighting.

If there was an answer to the riddle of life, I remember thinking that afternoon, I was no longer interested in what it might be. If the plan to reduce everyone's suffering was to define their needs without consulting them and then serve those needs, I did not want to be around. If to serve was to be free, I was gone.

That was the last meeting, the last international gathering for me of whatever it was we were— artists, writers, philosophers, theologians, historians. It was with a feeling of being released from long confinement that I gathered up Lora and our children and that we headed home. We stopped to see my parents in Amsterdam and Lora took the children on to St.-Denis to see their grandparents there. Once back in Detroit we sorted through all our belongings. In less than a week we reduced it all to six steamer trunks and some hand luggage.

Lora and I had thought about this a dozen times. When would we go? And where? She'd waited patiently for me to run the string out, to see we had to give our life and hope some different shape.

In that week of reduction we sold, consolidated, and gave away decades of work and personal possessions. We drove a rental truck to New York's West Side docks. We sailed to Belém aboard a freighter, with a South African crew and a Portuguese captain under a Liberian flag. Another boat, a riverboat, took us to Tucuruí—we might have taken a more direct route to our final destination, but it would have involved a wait. Like a flock of pigeons exploding from the ground at the approach of a cat, we had to go. Waiting anywhere now was unbearable. We took a truck across a stretch of the Transamazon to Santarém, then another riverboat, the last, four hundred miles up the Amazon to Manaus.

Lora and I had always thought if we had to go away—take what we called the geographic cure—it would be to Manaus. It turned out to be right, almost, so we were lucky. Lora died of dengue hemorrhagic fever eight years into it. I remained in Manaus another two years before moving six hundred miles up the Río Negro and the Curiouriari to Dowilda, on the Utala. Two of the children are still down there. The third, our youngest, is an activist with the Greens in Germany.

I initially came to Dowilda because in Manaus the memories of Lora were too many. I stayed because the Utala River country was a terrain and climate I could manage without too great a sense of defeat. Bands of Tukano helped me with a garden, with building the house, and with transport along the river and through the jungle. The Tukano and I had a similar, intense curiosity about life, but we approached living differently. One day, a few years after I arrived, I had altered the way I live enough that I could actually see what they called "the quiet," the realm of life that could not be sensed until one overcame the damage done to perception by a long exposure to inescapable noise.

Tukano country is directly on the equator. Makú live farther to the south. Nadobo downriver. What I have attained here is calmness, the calm behind a rock in an untenanted canyon. Do you know how an animal, an undomesticated animal, fights a cage? How it throws itself around so violently you think it must lack any sense of self-preservation? You feel sorry for it, but then when you have the power to open the cage and release the animal, you don't. Why? But what will happen? you ask. An animal like that, it might kill us. It doesn't understand—order is the reason it's in the cage to begin with. Without the cage, cruel as it may be, you argue, life would be too dangerous for the rest of us.

From my teenage years onward I was like a wild animal in a cage. Outwardly I demonstrated composure. I maintained this composure for months on end. I lived a life under control—not an unhappy life, not an unrequited life, but one measured off and paced by restriction. I did what was expected of me. I was not a rule breaker, a rabble-rouser. But the frantic turbulence, the desire to resist, was always loose inside me.

In my twenties I took every kind of legal antidepressant, every mood adjuster I could talk the doctor into, just to stay with it, to keep from going out the window of my room or sleeping through the whole day. I was holding on with both hands, perpetually seasick in an oarless boat, when I went to that meeting.

When Lora and I and the children were living in Detroit, my sense of hope came from four things. First, it came from what you might call the ordinary life of ordinary people in the neighborhoods around us. People with little money, occupying economic, social, and racial war zones, people with great resilience, great presence, a great capacity for joy. They had the ability to take advantage of every good moment, however it turned up. Hope also came to me from books I read written by people I'd never heard of but with whom I shared a politics. I seemed to share with them a premonition about impending disaster, which came from studying the aggressive interference in local life that Western businesses and their governments favor. I took hope as well from the power of poetry to meet misery with compassion. Finally, I found renewal in a circle of friends, at least one of whom, at any given moment, was of the view that all this would pass, that the nightmares would be turned back into the desert from which they had come.

A woman told me a story once, at a conference in Beirut, about her grandparents. They'd survived one of the death camps, Treblinka, I think. Many years after, her grandfather became a docent in a museum there, a guide. He led tourists through the ruins of the ovens, past the pits and the rusting barbed wire. What she admired most about her grandfather, she said, was that the purpose of his effort, as he explained it to her, was to warn. He did not volunteer to people that he had nearly died there. He would ask people, as if they were all relatives at the same funeral, to be vigilant, or it would come again. Sometimes, without knowing who it was they were talking to, people would break down, asking him for an explanation. He would try to comfort them.

He told his granddaughter that once a woman from Buenos Aires began shouting "*¡Nunca más! ¡Nunca más!,*" again and again. It kept exploding from her.

He held her. He rocked her. "Yes," he said, "that's it."

The trick, I suppose, is to contradict those who say vigilance is not necessary, while at the same time being careful not to declare any particular person or thing the enemy—that religion, this or that political party, a certain constituency, capitalism, this or that head of state. It would be to dismantle the stage upon which any tyrant, any self-anointed claimant to power, performed. It would be to direct the attention of his audience to a place where that tyrant has no authority, no influence.

Certain realities we now face—let me call some of them, collectively, biological, the narrowing of the biological possibility for human life because of large-scale atmospheric changes, falling supplies of fresh water, and the disruption of viral ecologies of the sort that produced the AIDS pandemic—transcend ideologies. They can't be dismissed out of hand or subjected to a compromise. To face them, let alone to find solutions to what they portend, requires a degree of imagination people have never had to exercise.

Or so we believe.

For myself, I want to live at Dowilda a while longer, until I can better understand the thing that makes the animal go crazy in the cage, and how to guard against it in every part of my life.

I love the feel of the sun's rays here, the seizure of my eyes by the trees. I love the outcry and song of the birds, the cavitation and susurration of the river. I love the fragrance of the air. I marvel at the sight of my hand emerging at the end of this blue cotton sleeve, drawing the world of which it is a part. I marvel that in the jungle of the upper Río Negro I can still recall the violence of politics in Manaus, the many reasons for despair in every city, but feel no loss of direction, no loss of belief in the power of people to imagine their lives in a completely different way. To imagine whatever lies beyond machinery.

I've had many months of back-and-forth with the Tukano. I'm intrigued by their stories of creation and their myths about the origins of all we see and smell and taste and hear around us. They are far more comfortable in a landscape of myth than people in the culture I'm from, though I'm not always at ease with their reasoning, their explanations. I'm gaited a different way.

I don't believe that the truths we search for, the ones that make us wise and free, fall, all of them, to any one group or time. My fascination with the Tukano is sustained by two thoughts. First, attention to the way they have chosen to live offers a perspective on humanity. My culture is of another time and place. What, then, can we say about the truths we seek that will be given deeper meaning by a consideration of each other's solutions? For example, do the Tukano still have a tool that my own North American culture threw away, centuries ago, but could now use, something as simple as a logic never known to the Greeks, nor to the Chinese or Sanskrit cultures?

And second, I have to admire how the Tukano remain in accord with the quiet world, their intercourse with what most of us separate out as the spirit world. For them, all things—the stars, the yatira on the jungle floor, the headwaters of the Utala—are immediate, open at any time to the solace that might come from holding a conversation with them. When I lie outside the house on a warm evening looking at the stars and feel comforted, and know this feeling is real even though it is beyond language, at least as I understand language, I'm not suspicious of the sense of peace I obtain. As the Tukano say, I am "speaking to the stars," the stars are responding, and the emotion of redemption I feel is just another form of my drawing, the result of uncalculating conversation with the elements of the world.

From time to time in the complicated realm of message exchange that stretches from the laptop to the hand-delivered letter, I hear from people I went to school with. Though it might be for the first time in twenty or thirty years, I find the conversations sometimes pick up where they left off. If we push beyond reminiscence and personal history, we can find where we once were. We share a respect for urgency. The experience of the intervening decades has not made these people despair or driven them to take refuge in cynicism. It has made them cautious, though, I would say.

Some years ago I got a letter from an old friend living in Urumchi, in Xinjiang, northwestern China. She'd gone with a friend of hers from Kashgar west to Tadshikistan, through Dushanbe to Baysun in southeastern Uzbekistan. At a place called Teshik-Tash they visited a cave where, fifty years before, a child buried by Neandertals 65,000 years ago was found. It had been an intentional burial, the child surrounded by pairs of ibex horns standing in defense. Shortly afterward, apparently, carnivores of some sort, perhaps hyenas, partially exhumed the body.

The threat of scavenging hyenas, if that's what kind of desecration they feared, did not deter the child's family from seeking a way to provide for its comfort. They tried to ensure that the child would not be disturbed. And then they traveled on.

Is it so different for us now? A hopeful people, attending to family tasks in a landscape of mysterious forces, a landscape where hyenas roam. We finish the day's work and move on, overland or into dreams, ever vigilant over the children.

When I read her letter about this burial, I had the breadth of time across which to consider our present tribulations, which she meant me to do.

They did not seem so tyrannical then.

My plan is to rest here awhile longer, then go down to see the children in Manaus. I want to send more drawings and field notes to the journals—I'm amused by the editors' suspicions, their disbelief about the shape and range of life here—and then make some significant gesture of gratitude to the Tukano for their hospitality.

They do not seem truly to lack, so it will be hard. Aweseela has asked me to leave a child, though I may have misunderstood this. In any case, I don't think I could manage such a thing.

I have a poem taped to a food tin in my house. It was written by a man named Zagajewski about, in his phrase, the need to embrace the mutilated world, to give in to a shared fate. The poem has kept me afloat, kept me from taking my own rationales too seriously, as though there could be no others.

It is a sobering truth that only with the greatest difficulty can we convey our life, our meaning, to other people. Some essence always seems to evaporate with the translation into language. I could write out a speech in Tukano that would sit well with everyone, the right words, the right tone of voice for the moment. I could demonstrate to my Tukano teachers what I have learned and in this way show respect for their skills. But our parting calls for something more.

I am not going to decide this alone. I'll put my suggestions before Aweseela. I am leaving, I will tell her, with many of their legends, stories about the origin of the world, and relationships between things in the world as they know it. Whether I understand the stories in every particular or not, I regard them as a kind of protection against what menaces every person—despair, conceit, failure of imagination. It is this feeling I want to give back: not *thank you* or *every blessing on you* but *I wish for my life to protect your life.*

I will not go until I have made a form of protection that fits into their world, something that says, as eloquently as their stories, *it is good to be fully alive* and *may this protect you against whatever it is in the world that cannot or will not see us, but that nevertheless has plans for us.*

I believe that it will be a story about Lora, how she carried the children and me when, blinded by a strange light, I thought I alone carried us.

> Eric Rutterman, indigenous rights
> activist, author, *Ishnalume, Kapanuna,*
> *Diltan Sa,* on leaving the Utala River
> country, to which the Tukano belong,
> nation of Brazil

Barry Lopez is the author of eight previous works of fiction and six works of nonfiction. His work appears regularly in *Harper's, The Paris Review, Orion,* and *The Georgia Review.* In addition to the National Book Award, he is the recipient of an Award in Literature from the American Academy of Arts and Letters, as well as fellowships from the Guggenheim, Lannan, and National Science Foundations. He lives in western Oregon.

Alan Magee is an artist of international repute whose works reside in many public collections, including at the Fine Arts Museums of San Francisco, the Art Institute of Chicago, and the National Portrait Gallery. He is represented by Forum Gallery in New York and Los Angeles. His work may be seen at www.alanmagee.com.